THASS A RUM OW JOB!

OW JOB!

More Tales of the Boy Jimma

Dedicated to my wife Pat, and all the members of my family. This is all part of their strange heritage!

THASS A RUM OW JOB!

MORE Tales of the Boy Jimma

by Tony Clarke

NOSTALGIA Publications

TOFTWOOD • DEREHAM • NORFOLK

Published by:
NOSTALGIA PUBLICATIONS
(Terry Davy)
7 Elm Park, Toftwood,
Dereham, Norfolk
NR19 1NB

First impression: October 1999

© Tony Clarke 1999

ISBN 0 947630 28 7

Design and typesetting:
NOSTALGIA PUBLICATIONS

Printed by:
PAGE BROS. (NORWICH) LTD.
Mile Cross Lane,
Norwich,
Norfolk NR6 6SA

Contents

Acknowledgements

With the publication of this book comes the realisation of a personal ambition which dates back to the time when I inherited a countryman's smock and began evolving the character of the Boy Jimma.

The stories which have adhered to me since then - much as flies stick to fly papers - have come, very much at random, from a variety of sources.

Thass A Rum Ow Job!, More Tales of the Boy Jimma, follows on, logically you might think, from Mighta Bin Wuss, Tales of the Boy Jimma, which was published last year.

The stories contained in the first book took the accident-prone Young Jimma from birth through schooling, marriage and a family to the point where he became Ow Jimma.

This publication deals with the second half of his life in which, instead of being a "sorft young tule," he has become a "sorft ow tule." In a week, as we say in East Anglia, he's still only about up to Wednesday night!

So now to my thankyous. First of all I must thank all those audiences who have had the good grace to laugh at the Boy Jimma on those occasions when he has been let loose at public functions.

Secondly, I must thank all those kind comedians who have "donated" jokes to me in public halls, shops, streets - where-ever we might have met, in fact.

Not least among these are my colleagues in the Press Gang, Keith Skipper's convivial company of travelling troubadours who tour the region dispensing mirth, wisdom and song in unequal proportions (there's more mirth than anything else!).

Thirdly, I must thank Terry Davy, of Nostalgia Publications, for keeping his nerve despite the knowledge that Mighta Bin Wuss could inevitably turn into Thass A Rum Ow Job!

Fourthly, I must thank my ancestors, and some of their friends and relations, who, when they posed all those years ago for the photographs which now fill a suitcase at my home, would certainly not have anticipated the use I have made of them. But I don't think they would have objected.

Finally, I must reserve my sincerest thanks for my family. To my wife Pat for not being too "miffed" about being asked to play the part of the Gal Liza (she's nothing like her, really), and for putting up with the Boy Jimma for all these years.

And to daughter Tina, elder son Jeremy and grandson Edward for again being such good sports in allowing me to use photographs for which they posed, and which were kindly taken by Peter Robins.

I am also grateful to all those good people who bought, and I hope enjoyed, Mighta Bin Wuss. I hope that little book, along with this one, its partner, will have been received in the spirit in which they were written.

That means a spirit of sincere affection and respect for the region of East Anglia and that fine race of "natives" who are indigenous to it. May their shadows never grow less.

"Whadda yew mean, corlin' me a indiggernant neartive!" Shut up, Jimma - just this once, please. I'm being serious!

Tony Clarke

Chapter 1 - **The Story so Far**

The memories which the Boy Jimma and his friend Jarge shared went back beyond those wartime days when the village station would be crowded with American GIs.

Picture the scene. You are in the bar of the Spoon and Spigot theme pub. A stained carpet covers the floor and mock-antique chairs, their seats covered by something which looks and feels like maroon velvet, surround small tables scattered around the room.

Curtains of similar material drape the windows, the all pervading aroma of nicotine and spilt beer clinging to them like an invisible shroud.

A bored looking barmaid languidly pulls at one of a line of multi-coloured pump handles ranged along the bar. Propelled by some kind of gas, the liquid hisses into a pint glass - another designer drink for a group of smart young things getting loudly merry on lager and "bloody marys".

The girls are on bloody marys, that is. At least, you assume they are the girls. They are the ones with the shorter hairstyles!

Just by the door a juke box, all chrome framed windows and crazy winking lights, makes its feeble but incessant effort to lure music lovers to part with their money.

Through the western saloon-style swing doors which give access to the restaurant you can just see a table of tourists wrestling with leathery sausages, greasy chips and baked beans.

These diners are not sufficiently "local" to have received advance warning of the horrors which masquerade as "pub grub" at the Spoon and Spigot.

Now I hasten to explain that this is not my general view of the typical English pub around the time the Boy Jimma entered the second phase of lifetime. Many traditional village ale houses were simply fading away, engulfed by a post-war tidal wave of gaseous mass produced beers, their passing - along with a long list of local breweries - lamented only by their dwindling bands of "regulars".

They were victims of their own remoteness. No longer able to survive solely on the patronage of their own parishioners, and accessible only by motor car, they were obliged to turn their gardens into car parks. Only to find that the understandable reluctance of the police to countenance drunken drivers on increasingly congested country roads kept those car parks half empty.

Other country pubs steadfastly retained their old names and traditions, pinning their hopes of long term survival on a return to the values of real ale and good food. And becoming, eventually, among the best places England can offer for "eating out".

At the end of the 20th century they are the last refuge of traditional English cooking, the final stronghold of the roast beef of old England - usually followed by apple pie or spotted dick!

For all I know, some may serve dumplings, and one day we may even see those traditional dishes, the "swede and swimmer" or the "beef patty", back on the menu.

But I dream. There was also a third category of village pub which faced the battle for survival with a desperate and pathetic belief that a change of name, a bit of carpet, a juke box and "live" music on Saturday nights would somehow give it a trendy image.

But it was a forlorn hope. And an Elvis number belted out in a phoney American accent by a bejewelled Saturday night singer - who worked during the week in the local chicken factory - signally failed to grip the audience with the same sense of awe as that inspired by "The King".

Much to Jimma's regret, the old Pig and Whistle in his village, the scene of so many happy gatherings in his younger days, had been an early victim of the decline of the traditional English village pub, had come under new management and a new name, and had taken this misguided and doomed survival route.

There was neither a spoon nor a spigot in sight. Gone were the barrels from behind the bar, the flagstones from the floor, the high backed Victorian settles and the open fireplace.

No longer did Sidney, the old landlord with the irritating twitch and the nasty habit of saying "Mighta bin wuss," preside over illicit games of "pokey die" every night and twice on Sundays when the church choir arrived after morning and evening service.

Sitting in the corner of what they had once known as the tap room, Jimma and his friend Jarge, the late developer and self-made wealthy businessman, looked a mite incongruous in these tatty modern surroundings.

They had just laid Jimma's father to rest and, in accordance with a family tradition going back many generations, our hero had inherited the old man's best country smock and had immediately been promoted from Young Jimma to Ow Jimma, the head of the family.

They had escaped from the family party which was in full swing at Jimma's little cottage. Distant aunts and uncles, who lived no more than 10 miles from his village yet had not seen Father for years and could barely remember what he looked like, had converged on his tiny cottage to mingle with the locals, drink tea, eat Suffolk rusks with lashings of butter, pork pie and ham sandwiches, and tell each other what a "good ow boy" the old man had been.

It was all rather too much for Jimma and Jarge. They, too, had not seen each other for years. Having drifted apart after the excitement of their youthful escapades, they wanted to have their own private reunion. They had much to talk about and were in reflective mood.

It was difficult to believe that this was the very pub in which Jimma's father had twice almost been involved in a punch-up. Once at his son's wedding and the other time when the butler from the Big House had inadvertently trodden in a doorway deposit left by Dinga Bell's dog, skidded over, clouted his head and wrongly believed Ow Jimma to have been somehow to blame.

Oh for those good old wartime days when Jimma's inglorious exploits had almost got him thrown out of the Home Guard, and when Huby's stories of ghostly monks, tunnels and graveyards had so delighted the Yanks on riotous evenings in this very room.

"Blast if this 'ere plearce wun't a soight better'n what that is now when I wus a boy," said Jimma, indicating his surroundings with a dismissive gesture. "There wus a time when yew cud cum in hare wi' the farmyard muck still on yar bewts an' nobodda'd gi' yer a second look. That wus jist loike bein' at hoom!"

Jarge grinned. "If thass what that wus loike yew musta hed a dattier hoom than what my Letitia keep," he remarked. "Still, I dew remember yew once sayin' yew cud never keep goats in yar bedrume 'cos they'd never be earble ter stand the smell!" "Shut yew up," responded Jimma. "I'd be rich dew I hed a quid fer evera time yew're cracked that one."

As friends together they had been undistinguished pupils under the jaundiced tuition of that stern disciplinarian, Mr Ernest Swishem, the village schoolmaster who expected to be addressed as "Sir" by all his pupils, present and past.

Jimma and Jarge had shared many adventures in their youth. They had been jailed for stealing potatoes when they were hungry, and Jarge would never forget their one disastrous fishing trip from Lowestoft when he had been saved from a watery grave in spite of - rather than because of - Jimma's clumsy rescue attempts.

They had sought their first job on the farm together, but while Jimma had somehow contrived to become a valued employee of the now elderly Farmer Greengrass, Jarge had resolved never to work for a master and had started on his own account as a small time dealer.

Matrimony had treated these two friends in different ways. While Jimma had enjoyed the homely charms and culinary skills of the Gal Liza, one-time cook at the Big House, the lovely Letitia Lavenham had shelved her ambitions to marry into the aristocracy and had settled for Jarge, a late developer who had made a fortune based securely on his singular ability to "reckon" without ever having been able to read or write.

By dint of hard work and some adroit wheeling and dealing he had built a good business and a fine home. Many a time, and in many a country saleyard, a barely perceptible twitch of his otherwise dour and expressionless face had been all he needed to attract the attention of the auctioneer and secure for himself a piece of land, a farm implement or an antique curio that he could sell on at a profit.

Meanwhile Jimma had toiled faithfully for Farmer Greengrass. Horses were giving way to tractors on the farm, the old binder making way for the combine harvester, and the stack yard where Jimma and Little Edie had spent so many happy and instructive afternoons, was soon to be a thing of the past.

Jimma and the Gal Liza still lived in one of his employer's cottages. To be precise, it was next-door to the one which had been occupied by Jimma's parents until the unfortunate episode of the exploding privy, and the unaccustomed bedroom exertions induced by the fire engine on that fateful Sunday morning, had caused Ow Jimma's sudden demise.

Now Mother would remain there alone, steadfastly adhering to the old ways of managing her daily work and highly critical of the Gal Liza when she aspired to possess any of "them new fangled modern machines" designed to make housekeeping easier.

At that very moment, as Jimma and Jarge were having their private reunion and finding even the tawdry surroundings of the Spoon and Spigot preferable to the row which was going on in Jimma's cottage,

Mother was holding forth to the mourners gathered in her parlour. "The trouble wi' young people terday is they're a-gorn sorft," she said pointedly in Liza's hearing. "They're allus wantin' a lotta things what we hed ter dew without.

"I din't hev no 'lectric boiler ter wash our cloothes in, nor yit no wireless ter listen to Warkers' Playtoime on. An' we hed ter manage on what Ow Jimma brought hoom from the farm.

"He wun't arnin' more'n about half a crown a week and nowadays I wudn't be surprised if Boy Jimma in't bringin' hoom four quid or more. They dornt know when they're well orf!"

"Dew anybodda want another cuppa tea?" asked Liza loudly, anxious to change the subect.

Privately, she was thinking: "Blast if I 'ont give Jimma a ding o' the lug fer creepin' orf an' leavin' me ter put up wi' har!"

By this time the conversation at the Spoon and Spigot had moved on to more personal matters.

Jarge's preoccupation with hard work and Letitia's unswerving devotion to elegant living meant that they had never had the time or the energy to produce children.

Even so, their one remaining ambition was one day to own the Big House, the ancestral home from which, in the old days, the aristocratic Lord and Lady Wymond-Hayme had ruled their large estate - and the lives of so many of the families for miles around.

Jimma had been an innocent youth, and despite the practical instruction generously given him by that notorious adolescent Little Edie, he had been a slow learner in the art of romance. He had been attracted to the Gal Liza mainly by her ability to cook apple pie and had married her after a clumsy though effective courtship largely conducted behind the churchyard wall.

They had managed to produce a son and daughter, despite Jimma's imperfect grasp of the basic procedures of procreation and his distinct suspicion that his daughter may have been the result of a dalliance between Liza and Sid.

The old landlord of the Pig and Whistle was now enjoying the peaceful eventide of his life in an old people's home, but Jimma's suspicions concerning his daughter's ancestry were based on the vaguely familiar twitch with which she was afflicted - and for which he could find no precedent in his own family.

Fuel was added to the smouldering cinders of doubt in his mind by the fact that although the mawther had been christened Jemima - this being the nearest female name they could think of to Jimma - the Gal Liza had insisted on giving her a second christian name, Cyd (pronounced Sid).

Jimma's missus was fond of going to the cinema in the nearest market town, and the odd choice of name, so she said, was in honour of a famous film actress of the day.

Beyond bestowing the occasional thoughtful look on his daughter, Jimma had never given voice to his doubts and they had continued as a happy and united family.

"That wus real noice ter see ow Sid at Father's fewneral," remarked Jimma as the memories flooded into his mind. "He reckon he dorn't git out much nowadays, an' a little trip out dew cheer 'im up."

"Yis," agreed Jarge. "He say thare's nuthin' like a good fewneral ter meet up wi' ow friends an' hev a bit of a mardle.

"I did hear tell he's quite happy in that ow hoom an' he hen't entirely lorst the arge for a bit a' female company, if yer know what I mean!"

"Oh ah," said Jimma suspiciously, remembering the old days when Sid had reputedly made strenuous efforts to justify his reputation for having an eye for the ladies. Remembering, also, how the Gal Liza, bored with his own moderate performance in bed, might well have been tempted by tales of Sid's much vaunted talents.

"He told me they dorn't half look arter 'im well in thet thare hoom," continued Jarge. "Evera night at bed-time they gi' him a choice between hevin' a cup o'Horlicks ter mearke 'im sleep or lettin' him look at one o' them film magazines wi' that picture o' Marilyn Monroe wi' har skart up round har wearst.

"Blast me, whadda he want wi' a picture o' Marilyn Monroe at his time o' life," exclaimed Jimma. "He must be earty-noine if he's a day."

"He say thet allus remind him o' the good times he used ter hev wi' orl them young mawthers whatta now grandmothers theirselves, and anyway he git excited and that stop him rollin' over an' fallin' outa bed!" explained Jarge without a hint of a smile on his craggy face.

"Well," thought Jimma. "Whatever Sid got up tew wi' the Gal Liza at least I know the boy Fred's mine."

Jimma could never forget the night his son had been conceived. "I wus jist a gittin' gorn when that there picture o' Greart Arnt Gertrude fell orfa the bedrume wall and clouted me acrorst the back a' the skull," he thought. "Blast if I din't see stars!" But he did not share the thought with Jarge.

For now the Boy Jimma must contemplate a future in which he would carry the onerous responsibility of being Ow Jimma, head of the family, official village idiot and pillock of the community.

And, to the diehards of the village, steeped as they still were in local tradition, Jimma's son would assume the title of Young Jimma - even though he had been christened Fred. That's how it was in the country.

Jimma stirred himself. "Well, I s'pose we better be a-gittin orf hoom dew the Gal Liza'll be a-gittin harself inter a mucksweat an' wantin' ter know what I're bin a-dewin on, an' yar Letitia'll be a-gorn shanny 'cos she're bin knockin' back too much Guinness."

"Are yew incinereartin' my Letitia drink tew much?" demanded Jarge indignantly.

"No," said Jimma with the hint of a twinkle in his eye. "But I wouldn't blearme har dew she did, hevin' ter live wi' yew orl these yare," he added as the two old friends left the pub and headed back to the cottage.

Note: Most of the incidents referred to in the foregoing chapter were related in all their glorious detail in *Mighta Bin Wuss, Tales of the Boy Jimma,* published in 1998 by Nostalgia Publications.

Chapter 2 -
The Village Football Match

Young Molly was a sprightly young mawther and the inspiration for Young Jimma's one disastrous attempt to play football

Jimma's son Fred - who will hereafter be referred to as Young Jimma to avoid confusion and to stick with family tradition - was as weedy a child as his father had been.

He also showed a similar lack of enthusiasm for school work, although he had inherited his father's love of nature and the countryside. This caused him to spend much of his time at school gazing out of the window of what he regarded as the prison of his classroom.

"He's just like his father," commented Ernest Swishem, now a portly figure of considerable authority in the village and nearing the end of his long career as village schoolmaster.

"He's tew bricks short of a load, if yew arst me," he added in accents which showed how 30 years in Jimma's village had undermined the original clarity of his diction.

There had been good news and bad news for Mr Swishem in the closing years of his teaching career. The limiting of class sizes meant that an assistant teacher had been appointed to the village school, a shy and earnest youth at the very start of his teaching career.

At the same time the raising of the school leaving age meant that children such as Young Jimma had to stay at school longer, although the setting up of secondary schools at least took them out of Mr Swishem's stern care at the age of 11.

When the time came for Young Jimma to go to secondary school in the nearby market town both his parents and Mr Swishem considered it a somewhat pointless exercise. It simply meant that he had to struggle with a wider range of academic subjects when his true talents suited him to an outdoor life.

He may not have been able to grasp the principles of mathematics or geometry, and the exact whereabouts of most foreign countries remained a mystery to him despite the endeavours of his geography teacher. But, from helping his father on the farm, he learned early in life how a straight furrow should be ploughed and how to milk a cow.

In the Jimma family the school summer holidays were still known as the harvest holidays for a very good reason - they all helped bring in the yield.

The other problem with school was that sport was obligatory. On the football and cricket fields Young Jimma, a gangly youth, displayed more enthusiasm for staying away from the action than talent for the game.

By and large, his parents were bringing up their children by a similar work ethic to that favoured by their own parents. Outside school hours there was work to be done in the house and yard, helping to milk the house cow and feed the pigs, chickens and rabbits. "Keep the little'uns busy an' they wo'nt hev toime ter git up ter mischief," was Liza's philosophy.

The upshot of all this was that Young Jimma had very little leisure time to investigate such sporting pursuits as existed in his village. And when he was able to escape his mother's watchful eye for a time, the only activities available to him were cycle speedway or football.

In the speedway stadiums of Norwich and Ipswich large crowds were thrilled by the skill and daring of international motorcycle stars who hurtled round the cinder track at great speed. At Carrow Road and Portman Road even larger gatherings roared on the heroic Canaries and the Blues.

The problem for the Young Jimmas of Norfolk and Suffolk was how to find the money and transport to get there. In the absence of both they spent long hours turning their rickety pedal bikes into machines fit to be raced on the makeshift tracks which they carefully laid out on any scrap of waste land they could find.

Race days were hair raising affairs, the riders pedalling like fury to the first bend and then leaning over and dragging their heels in the dust just like the professionals.

Collisions were frequent and many a rider ended up head over heels in the straw bales which acted as crash barriers. The sport became so well organised that, in its heyday, village teams competed against each other in leagues which were as well organised as the local football scene.

Many a race star returned home with scuffed shoes and torn trousers earning him forceful retribution from his indignant mother.

15

When they were not indulging in cycle speedway, the youths of Jimma's village turned out for their own football team which earned the nickname of "the Muckups" on account of its habit of playing, with much greater energy than skill, on a meadow normally occupied by cows.

The Muckups used an old leather ball which was so worn that the inflated bladder inside showed through the leather casing in places. The whole thing was held together by a lace which was invariably on the lower surface of the ball every time it descended from a great height.

For this reason, and because of the fact that it got very heavy after wet weather, when it quickly became caked with mud and cow dung, the Muckups avoided heading the ball any more often than was absolutely necessary.

To do so was to risk immediate concussion, and it was not unusual for dazed participants to be escorted from the field of play after inadvertently getting in the way of a full blooded shot at goal.

Their removal from the field was not so much for their own benefit as to prevent them from wandering about in an even more aimless fashion than they did when in full possession of their senses.

Once on the touchline they would usually be left largely unattended to regain consciousness while the action went on unabated.

The goals themselves were no more than piles of coats strategically dumped at each end of the field of play to serve as goalposts. Each game was therefore punctuated by furious arguments as to whether shots had actually passed between the "posts", over the non-existant bar, or wide of the target completely.

Young Jimma, being a delicate flower, rarely aspired to join the Muckups in their lusty endeavours. Indeed, his mother, anxious to protect him from what she considered to be undesirable company, would even go so far as to lock her son in his bedroom if she suspected there was any risk, however remote, of the Muckups persuading him to play. In this she was only following the practice which had been adopted by her mother-in-law. The old lady had been a strict disciplinarian in her day and was even now tempted to shout: "Go ter yar rume at once an' dunt yew show yar fearce 'till arter supper time!" whenever she fell out with Ow Jimma (the "Ow Jimma" in question being her son, and Liza's husband - as those who have managed to follow this narrative so far will already have deduced.)

There had even been times when both father and son had headed guiltily for their rooms when some misdemeanour had roused the womenfolk of the family. "Start as yew mean ter go on," Mother had advised the Gal Liza when she married the Boy Jimma. "He need a firm hand."

"Of course," she had added by way of kindly advice. "Yew dew know that orl men are the searme, dun't yer. God oonly giv 'em different fearces so we can tell 'em apart!"

However, the one ritual for which Ow Jimma and Young Jimma always managed to get out of the house together was the annual football match between their village, Much Snoring, and its near neighbour, Seething-in-the-Marsh.

A social and cultural gulf existed between these two warring communities far greater than the five miles which separated them. It had been bridged only once when a young woman from Snoring caused outrage by cohabiting with a young man from the neighbouring village.

Much against the better judgement of all concerned it was decided that, for the sake of decency, the two should get married. The local paper had recorded the historic occasion with the immortal headline: "Snoring bride for Seething man."

Apart from this, the annual football match, an unrelenting war of attrition, was the one point of contact between the inhabitants of the two villages. Knowing how tough these fixtures could get, even the Muckups displayed an unnatural reluctance to get involved.

Mr Swishem had been manager of the Much Snoring team for at least 27 years. He retained this important position on account of his being the only real figure of authority in the village now there was no vicar and Lord Wymond-Hayme had passed on to manage the Great Estate in the Sky.

Despite - or maybe because of - Mr Swishem's authoritarian approach to the game, it was often difficult to find enough volunteers to turn out for the village team.

It was always likely to be a bruising encounter, but at least the players got the chance to use a ball which was in slightly better condition than that employed by the Muckups. Even so, it still became remarkably heavy in muddy conditions and always came down lace first.

Although he admitted he was "scraping the barrel", Mr Swishem was forced, with great reluctance, to ask Ow Jimma and Young Jimma to make up the number. Ow Jimma accepted, but only because the team trained on a couple of evenings before the match and their training sessions were always followed by an hour or two in the pub. These were now the only evenings in the year when he could legitimately visit the Spoon and Spigot, and the only occasions when the pub was crowded these days.

Young Jimma would not have been in the slightest bit interested in the match had it not been for the fact that a certain young woman called Molly had attracted his interest, and she would almost certainly be among the spectators.

Molly was the daughter of a sprightly mawther who had once been well known to Ow Jimma as Little Edie. She was a popular girl, having inherited her mother's good looks, lively and generous personality - and her tendency to be liberal with her favours.

Young Jimma was convinced that Mr Swishem would prefer to keep him in reserve rather than expose his limited footballing talents on the field of play. The substitutes' bench, on which he would undoubtedly be seated, would be an ideal vantage point from which to make sheep's eyes at Molly.

To be honest, it was largely an unrequited love since Molly rarely showed even the slightest hint that she noticed Young Jimma's humble adoration. At the football match her attention would probably be drawn to more robust physiques, even though the Much Snoring team was not renowned for athleticism, and some of its players were well past their prime.

The sense of anticipation in the Spoon and Spigot that Saturday was similar to the tense atmosphere one might expect in the House of Commons prior to a declaration of war. From all parts of the bar voices could be heard discussing the impending battle and reviewing their team's chances of victory.

Everyone was an expert tactician, and the most knowledgeable experts of all were those who had prudently resolved not to take an active part in the proceedings.

Arguments raged on the merits, or otherwise, of various stalwart warriors. They were not in the least diminished by the fact that some of the warriors in question were in the room.

In fact, all the Much Snoring players and officials were there, with four notable exceptions. One was Mr Swishem, who was busy negotiating with a local farmer for the use of a pitch.

Also missing were Much Snoring's two "wing halves" who were still sleeping off the after effects of the night of debauchery into which the team's last training session had degenerated after Ow Jimma had gone home.

Young Jimma was also not on parade. He was still locked in his bedroom.

Harvey, the muscular individual who had once been the village blacksmith and was honorary captain of the Much Snoring team, pronounced judgement on all players who imbibed too freely before the match. "Bloody drunkards," he muttered as he pushed his empty tankard towards the barmaid, who automatically refilled it.

The time for the kick-off drew alarmingly near but nobody showed any inclination to betake himself to the field of play. There were two good reasons. First, Mr Swishem had not yet given any indication that he had succeeded in securing a pitch, and second, the visiting team had failed to put in its appearance.

Mr Swishem was, in fact, at that moment negotiating with a large herd of cows who seemed reluctant to give up their grazing rights. The goal posts, proper ones for this prestigious fixture, were already in position but cows are notoriously unsubtle beasts and these specimens were quite unable to accept the appearance of goalposts as a gentle hint that their field was required for a purpose other than grazing.

"Shoo," said Mr Swishem with the voice of authority. The cows stared curiously at him. "Shoo!" he repeated in tones which inspired fear and commanded instant obedience in the classroom.

The cows turned tale and wandered over to the centre of the pitch to continue chewing the cud, looking at Mr Swishem with that wide eyed innocence behind which all cows hide whatever thoughts occupy their bony heads.

Mr Swishem considered appealing to the beasts' better nature by means of music. Perhaps a melodic rendering of "Red Polls in the Sunset", as a tribute to their ancient breed, might lull them into a mood of co-operation.

The schoolmaster took one look at the meaningful expression on the face of the bull and discarded that notion.

Instead, he misguidedly decided that a good dose of discipline was what these cows needed. After all, it usually worked at school.

So he became impatient, demanding their obedience with threats of severe punishment. Six of the best, perhaps, or being kept in after milking to write out 200 times "I must do as I am told."

He would not only administer the cane liberally, he warned, but he would also inform their parents of their bad behaviour and they would undoubtedly be sent to bed without their evening feed.

Then Mr Swishem suddenly remembered that successive governments had softened school discipline, and punishments which he had favoured in his younger days were no longer legal. No doubt a similar softening up had occurred in the cowshed.

Needless to say, Mr Swishem's dire warnings had no effect on the cows. And at that precise moment the Seething-in-the-Marsh team appeared, riding along the nearby road on their bicycles.

"Hevin' a problem?" called their captain. "What do you think?" answered Mr Swishem with some truculence. "Too bad," replied the captain as he led his team off in the direction of the Spoon and Spigot.

Mr Swishem had hardly had time to reflect on the basic ingratitude of village footballers, especially the Seething-in-the-Marsh variety, when he heard a heavy and menacing thunder of hooves behind him, accompanied by some remarkably heavy breathing.

The farmer's bull, suddenly realising that Mr Swishem was attempting to evict him and his harem from their preferred field, had decided to take active counter measures. Mr Swishem needed no second bidding. Displaying a turn of speed more suited to an Olympic sprinter than a portly and elderly village schoolmaster, he set off in the direction of the road, the bull's hot breath giving him more incentive than all the gold medals ever won.

He accelerated towards the hedge that bounded the field, and leapt it like a ship in full sail breasting an Atlantic roller.

Being a firm believer in the academic pursuit of discretion rather than valour, he did not stop once he was on the road but set off at a lung bursting pace towards the Spoon and Spigot. His intention was to persuade all the footballers, friend or foe, drunk or sober, to return with him and assist in removing the cows.

Somewhat to his own surprise, he succeeded. But there was another surprise in store when this motley crowd finally arrived at the field on which battle was belatedly about to commence.

Chapter 3 -

Let Battle Commence

Dressed to impress, Young Jimma certainly looked the part before his one and only football match. But that was before the cows gained their revenge.

Mr Swishem could hardly believe his eyes when he and both teams arrived at the field of play. There was no sign of any cows.

There, where the touchline would be once it had been marked out, stood Young Jimma, Molly and about half a-dozen ancient rustics who constituted the "gate".

It transpired that Young Jimma, aware that his mother would frown on any liaison with a young woman, and that any attempt to engineer a "chance meeting" with the lovely Molly needed courage, care and cunning, had escaped through his bedroom window and down a drainpipe.

He might not know much about anything else, but one subject he did know about was cows and how to deal firmly with them. So, deploying the ancient rustics in much the same way that a shepherd would use his sheepdogs, Young Jimma had galvanised them into a determined and successful bid to drive the herd, including the bull, into a neighbouring field.

So far as Young Jimma was concerned, the best outcome of this little exercise was that Molly was much impressed by his unexpected and uncharacteristic display of leadership. In fact, she had actually noticed Young Jimma for the first time in her life.

The pitch was clear, the lines could be marked out, and the great match could begin. Everything was ready, including the referee.

Mr Swishem's shy young assistant had been "persuaded" by his head master to referee the game, and his neutrality was underpinned by the fact that he had inadvertently accepted drinks - and bribes - from both team captains who each now expected him to "fix" the game in their favour.

In consequence, he was fervently hoping for a draw. Let battle commence.

Then somebody remembered Much Snoring's two wayward wing halves who had still failed to turn up. Mr Swishem was faced with the indignity of asking the visiting captain if he could borrow one of their players so that the match could be played on a 10-a-side basis.

He was about to swallow his pride and make his approach when two of the ancient rustics, recalling that they had achieved "a fare ow tarn o' speed" in their younger days, rashly agreed to take the field if the home side was desperate.

The home side was desperate. But it was difficult for the visiting captain to stifle the sardonic smile which played around his lips as Much Snoring lined up with an elderly gentleman of determined countenance on each wing, muttering: "The old 'uns'll show 'em how ter play football."

A wag on the touchline didn't help matters much by calling: "Dornt yew run tew hard Charlie dew yar teeth'll drop out!"

"There in't no dearnger o' that happenin'," Charlie yelled back at him. "I're got 'em in me pocket!"

As the teams faced each other across the half-way line the pools panel, had it existed in those days, would hardly have forecast a home win. While the ancient rustics were glaring fiercely at their opponents, Young Jimma, picked to play centre-forward, looked at the giant centre-half who would be tackling him - if he ever got the ball - and decided that things definitely had not worked out as he had planned.

He hadn't expected to be playing at all, yet if he showed signs of timidity his chances with the "bootiful" Molly would be gone for ever.

The referee, being the only person in the village whose name had never appeared on the slate at the Spoon and Spigot - or the Pig and Whistle for that matter - took a coin from his pocket and tossed it in the air.

The two captains both shouted "hids", and then "tearls", and then: "Oh blast, mearke up yar mind," almost in unison.

To confuse matters further the coin landed on its edge in a cow pat and an argument promptly ensued as to whether it was "hids" or "tearls", and whether it mattered anyway.

When this was resolved the Much Snoring team found themselves facing down the slope but against the stiff breeze.

The referee pursed his lips, took a deep breath and blew a thunderous blast on his whistle. The game began - and at that precise moment two muscular village youths appeared and procleimed themselves to be Much Snoring's missing wing halves. The game stopped.

Now Mr Swishem became a rock upon whom burst a violent tide of abuse from the visiting team. Expressing loud and critical opinions about this further delay, the warriors of Seething-in-the-Marsh headed back in the direction of the Spoon and Spigot while Mr Swishem strode purposefully towards his two elderly substitutes.

The epitome of tact, he asked if they would kindly return to the touchline. He thanked them profusely for offering to help at a time when the civic pride of Much Snoring had been under such great threat, but after all, the younger men had been his original choice for the team and might be in less danger of sustaining a fatal injury from their exertions.

The reply he got was startling and said much for the stern stuff of which veteran Much Snoring villagers were made. Retarn ter the tuchloine? Mr Swishem could retarn ter the tuchloine if he bloody well loiked, but they wuz buggered if they wuz a-gorn tew.

Blast if they hent gorn ter orl that trubble a-tearkin' their coats orf, tuckin' their trouser legs in their socks and tearkin' out their false teeth which they had put in their pockets wrapped in handkercheeves. They wuz bloody well a-gorn ter play, and Mr Swishem cud wroite thet on his blackboard and swaller it!

"But you might get hurt," the schoolteacher protested, painfully aware of the great age of these two frustrated athletes.

"So we moight," agreed Charlie. "We moight cum over all of a mucksweat an' git carried orf in a box an' end up in the cimitry, but that 'ont matter a soight seein' as 'ow we're got more friends up there than what we're got left in the village, anyhow, so we'll hev plenty o' company. We 'ont be loonly.

"We're a-playin' an' thass orl there is tew it. Yew're gotta hev a bit o' excitement afore yew peg out."

Mr Swishem was faced with a terrible dilemma. While the argument had been going on the errant wing halves had gone behind the hedge to change into their football gear. Although still a bit bleary eyed from their over indulgence in "training", they were now ready for action.

The Seething-in-the-Marsh team had returned, its mood of incipient rebellion hardly improved by the discovery that the Spoon and Spigot had closed for the afternoon.

A pitched battle of words ensued, involving Mr Swishem, the two late comers, the aged reserves and the entire Seething-in-the-Marsh team.

The home team lolled about the pitch, helpless with laughter. All except Young Jimma who kept trying to think of sweet nothings to whisper into the newly receptive ear of the gal Molly.

The referee, a slight and studious figure wearing an old pair of Mr Swishem's shorts which reached well below his knees, attempted to intervene. "Perhaps," he ventured: "One of the old gentlemen might be prepared to play for Seething-in-the-Marsh. Then we could play 12-a-side."

"What?" screamed the rustics in unison. "Change sides? Be tarncoots? Play fer that lot? What are yew loike?" The referee retreated hurriedly.

In the end it was Mr Swishem's memory, his uniquely powerful position as village schoolmaster, and his formidable powers of persuasion that resolved the issue.

He recalled an occasion, a few months before, when he had caught one of the newly arrived latecomers, a youth called Ezra, "scrumping" apples from his orchard. Mr Swishem had duly read him the riot act, giving him several well aimed thumps for good measure.

Ezra, who had only recently left the village school and had personal experience of Mr Swishem's strict code of conduct, had pleaded with the schoolmaster not to tell his Dad who would undoubtedly give him a good "larruppin" with his leather belt.

Mr Swishem was not noted as a man of gentleness and tender understanding, but it suited his purpose to comply with the repentant Ezra's plea. After all, the boy would owe him a favour which, at some moment in the future, he would be able to call in.

That moment had arrived. Mr Swishem took Ezra aside. "Unless you play for Seething-in-the-Marsh I'll tell your father you've been scrumping apples from my orchard," he whispered threateningly.

Ezra went pale. Whatever happened he was in a no-win situation, as the Americans called it. Play for Seething-in-the-Marsh and his reputation would be for ever destroyed in his home village. He would have to move out.

Refuse to play for them and he'd be in for a hiding from his Dad, a hiding made worse by the interval of time which had elapsed since the crime. The former option was probably the lesser of the two evils.

The danger of becoming a target for assault and battery by the home team and spectators every time he went near the ball could be overcome by the simple expedient of staying as far away from it as possible throughout the game.

Somehow Mr Swishem's formidable powers of persuasion proved more effective with the Seething-in-the-Marsh captain than they had been with the cows. Ezra was accepted into the team, but only because the players were becoming rudely impatient over the delay, and their rising anger was being forcefully directed at their leader.

So the match finally began with 12 players on each side. Much Snoring, vociferously encouraged by their supporters, sailed into the attack. The blacksmith sent in a barrage of tremendous shots which, being well wide of the goal, brought no more reward than a hail of insults from the visiting goalkeeper who was getting tired of retrieving the ball from the long grass of the next field.

Much Snoring's players, their pent-up energies now let loose, were so intent on all-out attack that they hardly noticed the strengthening breeze against which they were playing. From one of the visitors' multitude of goal kicks the ball sailed into the air and, caressed by the mischievous wind, needed only one bounce to fly over the home goalkeeper's head and between the posts.

Since the goals were not equipped with nets the home supporters felt justified in doubting volubly the referee's award of a goal. But the ball had so obviously passed through the centre of its gaping mouth that the timid official risked being lynched by the visitors if he disallowed the score.

Much Snoring's strategy was now based on the simple ambition to score at all costs. The blacksmith let fly with another mighty shot which just happened to be a bit nearer the target than its many predecessors.

The visiting goalkeeper prepared to fetch the ball from the next field again, and had already departed on his mission when an aged spectator standing near the goal, moved with a speed which belied his years, shot out his walking stick and deflected the ball inside the post.

"Goal!" roared the home team and spectators alike. The referee, suddenly remembering his obligations to both teams, felt it was time the score was evened up. Screwing up all his courage he pointed to the centre spot - one goal apiece.

The visiting team was incensed. Its players surrounded the referee menacingly, but that newly confident official, looking to the touchline and seeing the expression of approval on the face of Mr Swishem, commendably stuck to his decision.

The Seething-in-the-Marsh captain was eventually obliged to convince his players that they could still defeat Much Snoring, even with the referee on the home team's side.

Much Snoring, bolstered by this unexpected turn of events, almost took a half-time lead. But the attempt ended in disaster and an early bath for Young Jimma.

The lad suddenly found himself five yards from the visitors' goal with the goalkeeper out of position and the ball at his feet. The goal yawned invitingly. His moment of fame had arrived; his chance to impress the gal Molly. He determined to make his scoring effort spectacular. He succeeded.

Drawing back his puny right leg in a mighty arc, he put the full force of his weedy frame (nine stone wet through) behind the kick. The "crowd" was poised for a mighty roar.

A fleeting vision passed before Young Jimma's mind's eye. It featured a crowd of jubilant Much Snoring players carrying him shoulder high from the pitch, the gal Molly all starry eyed with adoration and smothering him with kisses as he was set gently down at her side.

His foot sailed up to a height which would have done credit to a ballet dancer. He pirouetted on the other leg with commendable showmanship - and landed flat on his back in front of the goal. The ball remained stubbornly beyond the reach of his flailing feet.

The cows had gained their revenge. Young Jimma had landed in a large dollop of cow muck and now exuded an aroma which could most politely be described as "essence of farmyard".

Suddenly he became persona non grata with the rest of the home team for missing a "sitter". Even worse, the gal Molly took one look at him, laughed uncontrollably and held her nose expressively.

Miserably he picked himself up, slunk off the field and went home to face the wrath of his mother. "Where ha' yew bin?" she demanded, giving her son a sharp "ding o' the lug".

"An' time I think onnit, how did yew git outa yar bedrume? I'll hatta lock the winder next time as well as the door."

Stripped of his malodorous clothing, Young Jimma was taken to the pump in the back yard where, with his mother vigorously pumping the handle, the ice cold water cleaned him, gave him a lifelong aversion to village football, and temporarily cooled his ardour for the gal Molly.

Meanwhile, back at the football field, much of the spirit had gone out of the home team and Seething-in-the-Marsh had gained such a grip on the game that the ball had whistled through Much Snoring's goal about 12 times.

The referee, becoming alarmed that his hopes of a draw seemed extremely unlikely to be fulfilled, was more preoccupied with sorting out a possible means of escape than with controlling the game and keeping the score.

However, Providence favoured him in a most unexpected form. From the adjoining field, to which he had been banished under Young Jimma's direction, the bull had been watching the proceedings with undisguised hostility. Now his patience was exhausted and he led his following of cows in a determined bid to regain their rightful pasture.

At the start of the afternoon, Young Jimma, in his eagerness to impress the gal Molly with his ability to move the herd, had forgotten to shut the gate properly. Now the bull dislodged the five-barred obstacle with a disdainful flick of his horned head. A day which had started with such high hopes was ending in disaster for Young Jimma's already feeble reputation in the village.

With nostrils flaring and eyes ablaze, the bull surveyed the combatants on the football field. Picking the one apparent figure of authority, he made straight for the referee.

Instantly that official blew the final whistle, declared the game abandoned owing to a pitch invasion, and disappeared over the hedge - and straight into a particularly uninviting ditch.

The result being declared void, the players of both sides repaired to the Spoon and Spigot, now open again, and old feuds were slowly forgotten as the evening progressed.

The ale flowed and the company was regaled with songs and anecdotes from the ertswhile footballers. The village elders declared that never, in all their years, had they seen inhabitants of the two villages on such good terms.

They rubbed their old eyes in disbelief at the sight of the blacksmith and the Seething-in-the-Marsh captain clasped in a drunken embrace and giving infinite feeling to a raucous rendering of an obscure East Anglian folksong whose words were virtually unintelligible - and most certainly unprintable in a respectable volume like this.

A truce had been declared, at least until tomorrow. But back home Young Jimma knew nothing of this. Wrapped in a towel, his skin reddened by a liberal application of disinfectant and pummice stone, he sat miserably by the fire while his interfering grandmother, insisting that the old ways were best in times of "emergency", took his clothes next-door and boiled them in her copper.

The gal Molly? Well she just laughed about it all as the studious and quietly spoken referee, his pockets lined by the bribes he had accepted from both team captains, and which they had forgotten, came knocking at her door that night.

Would she like a ride in his pony and trap? Perhaps a drink at a nice quiet inn, if her mother didn't mind? Maybe the Hare and Hounds at Seething-in-the-Marsh? There'd be nobody there tonight!

It would be ideal for a nice quiet chat, just the two of them. He'd get her home before 10-o-clock.

So the man with the money got the girl. 'Twas ever thus!

Oh, and by the way, Ow Jimma sidled home late from the Spoon and Spigot that night - and a little the worse for wear. Neither his mother nor his wife spoke to him for a week. He remarked to himself: "Thass roight peaceful round here. If this here's a punishment I'll hatta mearke a habit o' stayin' out leart!"

Chapter 4 -
The Legacy

Felix, the former butler at the big house, acquired a certain style and swagger after being named as chief beneficiary in Lady Wymond-Hyme's will

Fred - alias Young Jimma - was as wayward a youth as his father had been before him, and after leaving school his efforts to find work were not graced with great success.

He was going through a mildly rebellious phase. Ow Jimma and the Gal Liza simply did not know what to do with him.

"He may ha' helped milk the cows an' orl that thare, but he dornt seem ter want ter git a proper job," complained Ow Jimma one evening as he and the Gal Liza discussed their son with Jarge and Letitia. "He 'ont cum longa me on the farm even thow the Marster tell him he can hev a job on account o' the long sarvice I're dun."

"Well I'd gi' im a job if he want one on account o' how long you an' me ha' bin friends," replied Jarge. "He can wark on one o' my farms."

"I dornt know what sort of a warker yew'd be a-gittin 'cos he dornt dew what his mother tell 'im tew no more," said the Gal Liza.

"Th' oonly parson he tearke notice of is 'is gran an' thass oonly 'cos she's gorn orf har hid an' tell him orl kinds o' tearls about what this village wus like the best part of a tidy few yare ago. I wun't mind so much if some on 'em were true!"

"I mean ter say," Liza continued. "The boy keep a-sayin' he wanta start a-walkin' out wi' mawthers an' I keep a-tellin' on 'im thare's more important things fer 'im ter be a-thinkin' about at his earge."

"He're tried orl sorts o' jobs but he dornt seem ter last more'n five an' twetty minutes afore he git kicked out fer dewin' suffin he din't orta."

Despite the bad publicity bestowed on Young Jimma by his parents, the outcome of this conversation was that Jarge repeated his offer of a job for the boy.

Jarge had made a success of his life. He had steadily built up a large portfolio of properties, including several houses which had formerly been in the hands of the aristocracy.

Now, as Lady Wymond-Hayme, that most elegant of them all, had recently followed His Lordship to the celestial estates, Jarge was close to realising his great ambition to own Much Snoring Hall, the Big House in his own village. He would sell off all his other properties for the chance to own that one.

By contrast, Jimma had led a life of unremitting labour for Farmer Greengrass. He was not only an independent man but also a loyal and contented employee. So he had consistently refused all offers of employment from his old friend Jarge on the grounds that he had always been happy working for "the Marster". Anyway, it would be like accepting charity, and there was no way he would ever do that.

Gal Liza had often disagreed. "Yew cudda arned a lot more money fer us warking fer yar ow frend;" she had said. "Stop yew a-mobbin' on me woman!" was all the response she had ever elicited from Jimma.

Now she took her chance. "If yew wunt go an' wark for ow Jarge, thare en't no reason ter stop Young Jimma gittin a job wi' 'im."

So it was decided. Young Jimma accepted employment with his father's friend, but only because to have refused it would have been to ensure that his parents would be "on his back" for the rest of his young life.

He was an odd boy who had inherited his father's basic and simple turn of phrase. He was on his way home after attending his job interview at Jarge's house when the vicar cycled into view.

It was a Tuesday and therefore the turn of Much Snoring to enjoy a visit from the young cleric who now shared his time between six parishes. "Hello, my boy," he said cheerily. "And where are you going?"

Young Jimma was in an uncommunicative mood. "I int a-gorn nowhere," he replied. "I'm a-comin' back!"

There being little chance of a fruitful conversation with this errant youth, the young vicar hopped back on his bike and pedalled off to his next call, thinking as he went: "I shall never understand these rude country people."

A week later Young Jimma was leading a cow along the village street when Mr Swishem hove into sight. Although he knew something of Young Jimma's prowess with cows, it still seemed odd to see this large and powerful beast being led by such a puny scraggy youth.

"And where are you taking that cow, my boy?" he asked with his usual voice of authority. "To the bull," responded Young Jimma succinctly.

"Does your father know about this?" Mr Swishem inquired. "That in't no good a-tellin' 'im," said Young Jimma. "The guvnor say thatta gotta be a bull fer this job!" "Insolent youth," thought Mr Swishem as he passed on up the street while Young Jimma continued innocently on his errand.

For a time Young Jimma worked in the carrot grading shed at one of Jarge's farms where the vegetables were sorted for different destinations - large for animal feed, medium for the shops, small for the canning factory.

But he was not suited to a production line task. His thoughts were constantly wandering and his mind dwelt so longingly on the great outdoors - just as it had done at school - that the carrots all went into the wrong boxes and Jarge received a letter of complaint from the canning factory.

"That boy's less use than the space he take up," said the foreman one day, unknowingly echoing a comment made by Mr Swishem many years before about the boy's father.

So it was that, by a curious twist of fate, Young Jimma was "lent" by Jarge to the head gardener at the Big House. By a roundabout route, he had succeeded in becoming under gardener there, a job for which his father had unsuccessfully applied 20 years earlier.

It suited Young Jimma ideally. He was not a great worker but he loved the outdoor life. He liked planting seeds and seeing the plants grow, even though, in his early days in the job, he could not entirely understand why two tiny seeds which looked the same should produce such different plants. Some turned into vegetables and some came up flowers.

But in time he grew to know them all, and to be able to identify all the wildlife he saw around him, including the many varieties of pests which attacked his seedlings.

He had found his niche in life, and provided he got on with his work, the head gardener largely left him to it.

Not long after he took the job all the staff of the Big House - the "outsiders" as well as "them indoors" - were called in for a conference. The Butler, who was at his formidable best, first instructed them to clean their boots before they were allowed inside, and then directed them into the unfamiliar surroundings of the dining room.

They sat nervously around the large refectory table, not knowing quite why they were there. Suddenly the door opened and a tall grey haired man wearing a dark suit and a superior expression on his gaunt face strode purposefully in and took his seat at the head of the table.

Mr Grabbitt, a senior partner in the local firm of solicitors, Sewe, Grabbitt and Runne, had arrived to read the Last Will and Testament of the late lamented Lady Wymond-Hayme.

Since the death of His Lordship some years before, she had been the last member of his ancient family to own this large estate which would now undoubtedly be broken up since there were no heirs.

Unaware of the historical significance of the occasion, Young Jimma quickly became bored and fidgetty as the austere Mr Grabbitt went solemnly through the convoluted preliminaries of the will reading.

In sepulchral tones, and speaking in capital letters without any other form of punctuation, the old solicitor revealed to the assembled company that he had in his hands the Last Will and Testament of the late Lady Cynthia Fiona Hortense Wymond-Hayme.

He informed them that the said Lady Cynthia Fiona Hortense Wymond-Hayme had vouchsafed herself to be "of sound mind" when drawing up her will on the umpteenth day of November 1947.

Young Jimma giggled. Turning to the housemaid, next to whom he was sitting, he said in a stage whisper: "I bet she wunt 'of sownd moind'. They say the ow gal went sorft afore she pegged out!"

If looks had been lethal Young Jimma would have perished instantly from the glares directed at him by both the Butler and Mr Grabbitt.

The latter cleared his throat meaningfully. "To continue," he said sternly. "Her Ladyship was not unaware of the 30 years of faithful service given to the family by Felix Potts, her butler, and in recognition of this she has bequeathed to him Much Snoring Hall and twenty thousand acres."

The Butler's dignified expression slipped only momentarily. "Of course I am most grateful to Her Ladyship," he said, directing a pious look towards the ceiling just in case Her Ladyship's soul had ascended somewhere in that direction.

"However, it comes as little surprise," he continued. "Many times during her lifetime did Her Ladyship remark, 'Felix,' (she habitually used my christian name after the death of His Lordship, you see); 'Felix,' she would say; 'You have served me well these many years. I must find some way to reward you.'"

The statement somehow reinforced the suspicions which other members of the staff had nursed - but never mentioned - that the relationship between the Lady and her Butler might occasionally have been as close as that between Lady Chatterly and her gamekeeper.

Which was why they had sometimes called him "Mellers" - but only among themselves.

Again Young Jimma could not keep his mouth shut. "Pompous ow tule," he hissed to the housemaid.

Again there was an uncomfortable silence. Again Mr Grabbitt cleared his throat. "What did you say, young man?" he asked. "Nuthin'," said Young Jimma, growing red in the face. "Nuthin' at orl."

"Any more interruptions and you will be thrown out," said the solicitor angrily. "For the moment we will continue."

"Her Ladyship was similarly appreciative of the 20 years' service given by Cook." He read from the document before him: "This service was especially commendable in view of the fact that Cook had to take up the position suddenly when her predecessor, an unfortunate woman called Liza, suddenly decided to throw her life away by marrying an uneducated and disreputable fool of a man." This quotation from the Will proved that Her Ladyship had never been able to forgive Ow Jimma for the occasion when he had inadvertently discarded his trousers whilst being interviewed for a job at the Big House. But that's another story. . . .

Cook, whose ample form was not unlike that of a ship's figurehead, though less indecorously dressed, seemed visibly to swell with pride.

"In recognition of Cook's faithful service Her Ladyship has bequeathed to her Little Seething Hall and ten thousand acres," announced Mr Grabbitt.

There was a loud crash as Cook fell off her chair in a dead faint. Mr Grabbitt was galvanised into action. He leapt from his chair and, crouching over the bulky form crumpled on the floor, he first considered giving her the kiss of life and then thought better of it.

Even in repose her face was no oil painting. Anyway, the fluttering of her moustache suggested that life was not extinct. So he contented himself by fanning the woman with Her Ladyship's Last Will and Testament.

As Mr Grabbitt, the Butler and Young Jimma all struggled to lift this horizontal heavyweight into an armchair, Young Jimma felt emboldened to ask; "And what dew yer think Har Leardyship hev left me in har will?"

"Sod all, I should think," declared the Butler. His normally impeccable Oxford accent was inclined to slip a bit in times of stress.

"Oh ah!" exclaimed Young Jimma, his eyes wide with excited expectation. "An' how many eacres go with that!"

"Get Out!" shouted the Butler and Mr Grabbitt together. "And don't bother to come back," added the Butler, having thus managed to banish two generations of the Jimma family from the Big House.

But Young Jimma had the last laugh. At times during his long and faithful service to Her Ladyship the Butler had found her a demanding employer. He was tired and in no mood to shoulder the responsibility of managing his inheritance.

At his time of life money was more attractive than status or responsibility.

A week after the Will had been legally executed Jarge met the Butler in the Spoon and Spigot, made him an offer, and secured the Big House at a bargain price. He still could not read or write - but he could reckon!

And the first thing he did, out of kindness to his old friend, was reinstate Young Jimma in the gardens.

Chapter 5 -
Ton-Up Kid

It wasn't the motorcycle accident which left Young Jimma injured but the first aid administered by Wally Hogg which gave him a permanent crick in the neck.

If Ow Jimma had hoped that job security and a regular income would calm Young Jimma down and make him less rebellious, he was to be sorely disappointed.

After the debacle of the village football match, Young Jimma had resolved to do everything he could to restore his battered reputation in the village, and in the eyes of the lovely Molly.

So he evolved a master plan, and each week he called at the post office, a special counter at the back of the village shop, to put some money in his National Savings account.

He knew he could keep this activity secret from his father who had an aversion to banks and was never seen in the village shop anyway.

Such slender financial reserves as Ow Jimma possessed were strategically hidden around his home. They consisted of a small amount of money sewn into the mattress on his bed and a slightly larger sum contained in an old biscuit tin buried in the middle of his chicken run.

None of this money gained any interest, of course, and the biscuit tin was buried sufficiently deep to prevent the chickens from turning it into a deposit account. But Jimma was fairly convinced that nobody, not even other members of his family, would ever guess where his worldly wealth lay hidden.

Gal Liza knew, of course, but she did not tell Ow Jimma. And Young Jimma had a shrewd idea that his father must be keeping money somewhere because he very rarely spent any.

Life was relatively self sufficient in the Jimma household. The house cow and a couple of goats were the source of milk, butter and cheese; all the family's vegetables were grown in the garden, the chickens provided a regular supply of eggs, there were rabbits to be caught around the farm, and the occasional slaughter of a pig produced ham and bacon.

Gal Liza was also a dab hand at making elderberry wine, a talent of which Young Jimma fell foul one night when he discovered her "wine cellar" in the pantry and sampled rather too much of the product.

That night there was some concern in the family when Young Jimma could not be found. Had he been kidnapped and sold off to the white slave trade? Ow Jimma soon discarded this thought on the grounds that Young Jimma had such a poor work record that he couldn't have fetched enough on the open slave market to make kidnapping him worth-while.

He had a quick look in the mattress. Then, since the night was dark and there was no moon, he took his spade from the shed and moved silently and furtively towards the chicken run. Well, you couldn't be too careful, and the boy just might have absconded with the money.

It is very difficult to do anything quietly in an occupied chicken run, even at night, and Ow Jimma's search for the biscuit tin aroused much cackling from within the chicken house.

Gal Liza, who had been visiting Mother in her cottage next-door, called from the back door; "Whass happenin' out thare. Go on, git orf if yew're a barglar. We dun't want intrewders around here."

"Thass orl roight my luv," called Ow Jimma with an uncharacteristic display of affection. "Thass oonly a ow fox arter the bads. I're sin him orf and locked 'em up. Dornt yew worry."

"Dew yer want any help?" called Liza, walking up the garden path. "No my dear, thass orl roight," Ow Jimma replied hurriedly as he replaced the biscuit tin in its hole and shovelled earth and chicken manure on it in the darkness.

"What are yew a-dewin' on diggin' about in thare?" inquired Liza, drawing closer and peering through the wire netting, determined to make mischief.

"Oonly clearin' up the chicken shi - sorry, muck - ter mearke the place look a bit tidier," explained her husband lamely. Gal Liza smiled her secret smile. "One o'these hare days I'll hatta hev a dig round in that thare chicken run," she said. "Yew moight hev a body buried in thare, or suffin."

At that moment Ow Jimma resolved that, at the earliest opportunity, he would find a safer place for the biscuit tin. Maybe the pig sty would be just right. Liza would never think to look in there.

Which is how Ow Jimma stumbled on the missing Young Jimma. As he peered over the pig sty wall, trying to assess the best location for the biscuit tin, his gaze alighted on his son.

The boy was blissfully asleep, his arms wrapped round the bulky form of Bertha the sow. "Oh Molly," Young Jimma whispered as Ow Jimma took hold of his sleeping son and pulled him none too gently away from the recumbent porker.

Young Jimma's eyes opened wide. "Where am I?" he inquired as two images of his father swam dizzily into view. "In the pig sty," they replied. "And why were yew a-callin' our ow sow Molly? Har nearme's Bertha."

"Blast, I never did - did I?" slurred Young Jimma thickly. He dimly recalled the beautiful dream he had been enjoying and then looked at the mountainous muck-smeared figure of Bertha, now snorting with belated indignation.

By now the two images of Father had resolved themselves into one, and he was wearing a sly grin on his weatherbeaten face.

"If yew're a-gorn sorft on the mawther Molly, I dun't fancy yar charnces of a long an' happy loife dew I tell har yew mistook har fer a pig," remarked Ow Jimma. "She're gotta temper on har, that one!"

"You wouldn't!" exclaimed the fearful Young Jimma. "I might dew," responded his father with a knowing wink: "Dew yew dornt staart a-mindin' yar manners and a-dewin' the things yar Ma and me arst yer ter dew. An' she won't be nun tew happy about yew a-gittin arter har elderberry wine, ow partner."

Gal Liza was, indeed, none too happy. She took Young Jimma by the scruff of his neck and propelled him into the back yard towards the dreaded pump. Pig muck may have had a different consistency from cow muck, but it smelled just as bad. Anyway, Young Jimma needed sobering up.

His clothes were quickly removed, and for the second time in a month ice cold water splashed over his puny shivering torso, reminding him again that life could be hard for a love-lorn swain.

It wasn't the cold shower that worried Young Jimma so much as his father's threat to tell Molly about his drunken "date" with a pig. He could just imagine the girl's laughing face as she told him: "If yew wus a-gorn ter be unfearthful ter me you mighta chosen somebodda a bit better lookin' than Bertha."

His already damaged image would be shattered for ever. And worse was to come the following morning when, waking with a heavy heart and an even heavier head, he was confronted by the smiling face of his mother.

"Yew'll be glad ter know I arnt a-gorn ter punish yew fer what yew dun last night," she said, in motherly fashion. "Thass 'cos a-what I hard from little ow Mrs Tinker what keep the village shop.

"She reckon yew're bin a-puttin' money in the post orfice an' I're allus taught yew ter be thrifty. That show yew're gotta a sight more sense than yar farther. He go diggin' hooles in his chicken run an' think I dornt know what he put in 'em".

Young Jimma would have been happy if his mother had left it at that. But she continued: "What are yew a-searvin' up for, son?" she asked solicitously. "Er, nothin' much," he replied. "Thass jist that yew're allus towd me to put suffin aside fer a rearny day an' evera time yew keep a-sloshin' pump water over me that feel like rearn!"

There was no way that Young Jimma could reveal to his mother the truth behind his regular investments at the post office. Convinced that he needed to steal a march over his rivals among the Muck-Ups for Molly's affections, he was determined to raise enough money to put a deposit down on a second hand Norton motor bike.

He had seen them advertised in the local paper, and he reckoned he had just about enough income to pay his deposit and then the rest at monthly intervals. He knew his mother would not approve. It didn't matter too much what his father thought. Anyway, the open road beckoned. If Molly, dazzled by the glamour of his gleaming machine, accepted his invitation for a ride on the pillion, she would need to cling on for dear life - and that meant putting her arms around him.

None of the Muck-Ups had motor bikes. He would be the trendiest youth in the village and everybody would look up to him.

Needless to say, it did not work out quite like that. Yes, Young Jimma bought his bike. Yes, his mother "blew her top". And yes, Young Jimma paid no regard to the stern warnings from his father that he would "come a helluva cropper one o' these hare days."

The rules of the road were not so strict in those days, and hi-tech crash helmets were things of the future. Young Jimma had cleaned out his savings account. He had acquired the bike, a provisional driving licence and the "L" plates that went with it. Now he was keen to get on the road, despite having no savings left for protective clothing.

"If yew must, I s'pose yew will," said Ow Jimma, resigned to the situation. "But p'raps these'll help." He handed Young Jimma a flying helmet and goggles which had been left to him as a souvenir by one of the Americans who had served at the "camp" during the war.

Young Jimma was impressed. He gave the bike one final polish, donned his helmet and goggles, and kicked the machine into life. The Norton's throaty roar was heard throughout the neighbourhood as he rode proudly along the village street, first to the cycle speedway track, and then to the football ground, in the hope of impressing any passing Muck-Up, and finally to the front gate of Molly's house.

"What the hell's that duller," exclaimed her father, woken from an after dinner sleep by the sound of Young Jimma revving the engine importantly. Molly rushed out of the house. "Stop thet row at once," she commanded: "Dew Father'll hev yar guts fer garters an' he'll gi' me a good larruppin fer hevin' such a rowdy boyfriend - an' he dornt loike me hevin' boyfriends at all."

Young Jimma, suddenly full of manly confidence, replied: "I'll stop the row dew yew promise ter come out longa me fer a bike ride arter tea."

"Orl roight, orl roight, but switch that thing orf now. An' dornt come back hare ternight; I'll meet yer outside the shop," responded Molly as she hurried back into the house, leaving Young Jimma to push his silent bike round the corner.

In order to get out of the house for an hour without facing too many awkward questions, Molly would have to tell her father that she was meeting a girl friend.

Once out of earshot Young Jimma kicked the Norton into life and sped up the loke towards Farmer Greengrass's farm. Chickens scattered in all directions as he roared around the barn and screeched to a halt outside his father's cottage.

Suddenly Young Jimma found he was shivering. Riding a motor bike was a colder experience than he had expected. It certainly would be when his puny frame was subjected to the rush of the night air.

So, having rummaged around in his own sparsely filled wardrobe and found very little of any use, he asked his mother's advice.

Liza, also resigned to her son's love affair with the Norton - "He'll sune grow out of it," Mrs Tinker had assured her in the village shop - agreed with her son. "Yis, I dun't doubt that'll be a bit rarfty ternight," she said, producing a large waistcoat belonging to Ow Jimma.

"Dew yew put this hare weskit on over the top of what yew're got on already," she said. "Oonly, seein' as how orl that wind'll be a-comin' from the front, I reckon yew'd best put it on back ter front so yew dun't git a drarft threw orl them buttonhooles."

While all this was happening Ow Jimma was up at the farm checking the stock and making his apologies to Farmer Greengrass. "Six o' yar hins ha' stopped layin'," he said.

"Oh ah, how der yew know?" inquired the old man. "I'm sorry ter say my son runned over 'em!" explained Ow Jimma, offering some money by way of compensation.

"An' blast if he din't mearke a helluva row time he wus a-dewin onnit," said the farmer. But he waved away Jimma's money and said no more.

So Young Jimma set off, wearing his flying helmet and goggles, and his father's "weskit" back to front. Molly was most impressed. "I see yew're well protected agin the wind," she remarked as she hopped on the pillion seat and put her arms around Young Jimma's unusually bulky form.

They set off and went for a ride along the country lanes. Even the cows looked up in surprise as Young Jimma and the gal Molly roared past.

By the time Young Jimma decided to head back towards the village he was gaining in confidence and anxious to impress his passenger with the Norton's capabilities. He was to regret succumbing to this temptation.

He steadily increased speed and by the time he raced round the sharp bend between the Spoon and Spigot pub and the village pond he was at full throttle.

A mother duck was leading her seven ducklings across the road. There was a screech of brakes, a squeal of tyres, and the bucking bike pitched Young Jimma over its handlebars, landing him insensible beside the road.

Poor Molly fared even worse. As the bike reared she was sent flying over Jimma and head first into the pond. The duck calmly gathered her brood around her and launched them on to the ruffled water.

The door of the Spoon and Spigot burst open and out rushed Jarge and Wally Hogg, who ran the local boar service. "I'll go arter the gal an' yew deal wi' Young Jimma," commanded Jarge. "Yew're got plenty o' experience o' givin' the kiss a-life ter runts!" he added as he waded into the water and grabbed the girl.

By the time the ambulance arrived Wally was crouching over the seemingly lifeless form of Young Jimma. "Thass a duzzy good job yew got here quick," Wally told the ambulance man. "I wearsted valuable time tryin' ter tarn his head the right way round afore I realised he're got his weskit on back ter front! I dornt think thatta dun 'im much good."

But the boy was breathing so the ambulance man turned to Jarge. He had pulled Molly half way out of the water and was pumping her diaphragm vigorously. Each time Jarge applied pressure water gushed from her spluttering mouth.

"Move over," said the ambulance man, pushing Jarge out of the way. "I think yew'd better stop a-dewin' that afore yew pump the pond dry!"

Fortunately, both rider and pillion passenger escaped with no more than concussion and a good hiding from their parents. Mind you, Jimma couldn't understand why he was suffering such a severe crick in the neck as he went to the kiosk on the village green to telephone the garage from which he had bought his prized Norton.

"I're gotta problem wi' that bike what yew sold me," he told the man at the garage. "Dew yer think yew cud come an pick it up?"

"Where from?" asked the garage man. "The middle o' our village pond," replied a chastened Young Jimma, now resolved to give up biking - and the gal Molly - for ever.

Chapter 6 -
The Nuptial Stakes

Young Jimma, proudly wearing the family smock, made a handsome "catch" for the Gal Elsie.

Time went by and Young Jimma and his sister, the gal Jemima, were approaching marriageable age. Neither of them, however, were regarded by other families in the village as a particularly good catch.

The world at large was unaware of the riches which lay hidden in Ow Jimma's pig sty, staunchly guarded by the redoubtable Bertha, and neither Young Jimma nor his sister were among the most beautiful young people in the neighbourhood.

Young Jimma's brief flirtation with motor bikes had left him with a tendency to lean over to one side and to give the impression that he was always looking over his shoulder.

His strangely furtive demeanour was due, not so much to the accident as to the misguided first aid administered by Wally Hogg after it.

Jemima, it seemed, inherited her looks from her father and her ruddy complexion from her mother. The unfortunate twitch with which she had been afflicted since birth tended to make her a shy girl.

The overall effect of these afflictions was that neither Young Jimma nor Jemima could look a person straight in the eye; not for long, anyway.

"They reckon bewty is skin deep," remarked Ow Jimma to the Gal Liza one day, vaguely remembering something he had heard at Sunday school years before.

"Some people ha' got bewty in their innermoost selves," he added, waxing strangely poetical.

"If that's the cearse, I think we orta try tarnin' our kids inside out," retorted the Gal Liza.

But, as is so often the case in life, the train of events which was to change their children's fortunes was set in motion when Ow Jimma and the Gal Liza least expected it.

Ow Jimma was on his way home from work one Wednesday afternoon when, quite by chance, he met the woman he had once known as Little Edie. In her day she had been a "flighty piece" and free with her favours.

"Blast bor," she greeted him: "How are yer a-gorn on? I hent sin yew fer a tidy while."

"Fair ter middlin'," said Ow Jimma. "Yew know, I keep a-jammin about, puttin' one foot in front o' th'other."

"Blast me, yew wus cearpable of a bit more'n that when yew wus a boy," recalled Edie. "Dew yew remember them Wensdy arternunes we used ter hev in the stack yard?"

Embarrassment began to turn Jimma's already red face an even higher colour. "Well, I s'pose yew tried ter teach me a trick or tew," he admitted. "But that never dun me much good arter I got married."

"I dunt s'pose that did," agreed Edie. "Yew wunt a lotta cop, I're gotta admit. But in't that strange. Here we are on that same bit o' road yew used ter walk home along, an' if my memory sarve me well that bit o' field over there wi' them cows innit and the fence round is where the stack yard used ter be.

"Won't that be a larf dew we slipped down ahind thet thare fence an' hed a little kiss an' cuddle, jist ter remember the owd times, so ter speak?"

"What'd the Gal Liza say?" said Jimma, protesting and drawing back with vivid memories of the day his father had caught the two of them coming out of the stack yard.

"She dornt need ter know," answered the persuasive Edie. "An' that dornt hatta lead ter nothin' more serious. I're gotta husband an' five kids now, anyway."

"I shud think yew're hed enough o' kissin' an' cuddlin' then," replied Ow Jimma. But reluctantly he allowed himself to be led into the field. The two old friends sank down behind the fence.

Edie wrapped her eager arms around Ow Jimma and their lips met in a shuddering kiss which seemed to last for ever. A strange sensation rippled through Jimma's ageing body.

Eventually Edie came up for air. "Blast if I know!" she exclaimed. "Yew hen't harf improved since yew wus a boy. That kiss sent a shiver up an' down my spine."

"Thass probly 'cos this hare fence what we're up agin wun't electrified in them days!" said Jimma, suddenly aware that the strange sensation had been inspired by the low current in the wire which passed along the fence. Sadly, it was not a sign of an awakening libido. "The farmer ha' gotta keep the cows in the fild somehow," he said.

"Never mind what that wus," said Edie. "Let's try it agin." And they did, with the same result.

"That don't harf remind me o' when I wus young," said Edie. "I think we orta git tergather agin of a Wensdy afternune."

Jimma was worried. Knowing what a spirited mawther she had been in her day, he was also aware that Edie had married the village undertaker, Hector Boddy.

Although Hector had given her five little 'uns, Jimma could well imagine that she had yearned for a livelier life than one lived in such close proximity to a chapel of rest.

"I wouldn't like the thought o' orl them dead people livin' at the bottom o' my garden, so the Lord only know what she think onnit," Jimma thought to himself. "P'raps she want a bit of a fling afore she end up in the chapel o' rest harself."

But his fears were groundless. "Dornt yew worry," said Edie, noticing the frown on Ow Jimma's face. "I oonly thought we cud hev a family git tergather one Wensdy arternune.

"Yer see, I're got this gal, Elsie, whass a bit lively an' I'd like ter git har hitched ter settle har down a bit."

Jimma's mind dwelt, for a moment, on the multitude of sins which the phrase "a bit lively" could cover when used by someone like Little Edie to describe her own daughter.

"Yew're gotta son, I believe," she continued, showing a devious streak which Jimma well remembered from her younger days. "Dew yer think we cud git 'em tergather?"

When Jimma got home he faced an inquisition in stereo from his wife and mother. "Where ha' yew bin, boy? Yar tea's a-gittin' cold," they chorussed. It was just like old times.

He was grateful for the chance to divert their attention by offering a proposition which they just might welcome. "I carnt think any kid o' Edie's 'll be much cop," said Mother. "But then, yew did wanta git that boy o' yars orf of yar hands.

"He is a bit of a tule, jist like his farther wus afore 'im," she added unnecessarily, or so Jimma thought.

So the family tea party took place the following weekend. It was a resounding success despite the fact that Edie's husband could not stop talking about beautiful funerals he had attended. "Yar farther's wus one o' the best," he assured Ow Jimma in what was intended as a compliment.

Ow Jimma was prepared to put up with the conversation, knowing that Young Jimma had taken the Gal Elsie down the garden path to look at his Brussells sprouts.

"How'd yer git on?" he asked his son after their visitors had gone. There were stars in Young Jimma's eyes. "She's suffin wunnerful, Father," he confided. "I'm a-tearken har out ter the pictures next week an' we might go ter the chip shop arterwards!"

The appointed evening arrived and Young Jimma set off with the Gal Elsie, on their bikes, heading for the picture house at the nearby market town.

Young Jimma's carefully worked out budget for the evening only allowed them a visit to the chip shop if they sat in the cheapest seats at the cinema - right at the front.

The physical discomfort of staring upwards at the enormous screen bothered Elsie more than it worried Young Jimma who had a permanent crick in his neck, anyway. So Elsie's attention wandered. Her arm stole along the back of the seat and around Young Jimma's shoulders. They had eyes only for each other.

The chip shop was ahead of its time for the variety of menu it offered. Along with the plaice, haddock and sloppy peas, there were pies, sausages and many other appetising items.

"What dew yer fancy?" asked the saucy young girl behind the counter. "Haddock, plaice or a bit o' slap an' tickle?"

Elsie looked sideways at Young Jimma. "I'll hev a quickie," he said. A well aimed blow from the spirited Elsie caught him flush on the lug.

The furious girl turned and was on her way out of the shop when the young schoolteacher, Mr Swishem's deputy, who was waiting in the queue, caught her by the arm. She turned, and seeing who had detained her, resisted the temptation to wrench her arm free and disappear into the night.

"I think the pronunciation Young Jimma intended was keesh," said the young man gently. "Spelt Q-U-I-C-H-E," he added, pointing at the menu.

Elsie's indignation subsided. She looked back at the counter, where Young Jimma was rubbing his ear ruefully, and took pity on him. Anyway, he was her only chance of getting a meal tonight.

They both decided to stick to what they knew - fish and chips. And as they left the shop Young Jimma whispered a heartfelt "Thanks" to the schoolmaster. "Don't mention it," replied the young man, smiling quietly.

As they biked home, past Greengrass's farm, they came to a fenced field. "Shall we stop a while?" asked Elsie. "Arter all, yew did say yew wanted a quickie!"

The two sank down behind the fence at the spot where, unknown to them, Young Jimma's father and Elsie's mother had enjoyed many an amorous moment.

Young Jimma's performance was supercharged. Electricity flowed between the young couple. "Blast me!" exclaimed Elsie eventually: "Yew hin't harf got hidden talents! That seem like we cud git on well tergather."

Will yer marry me then?" asked Young Jimma, striking while he was still switched on and plugged in, so to speak. "I jist might," replied Elsie, giving him as definite an answer as any East Anglian should expect.

The wedding took place six months later, but after the initial excitement Elsie found marriage to Young Jimma disappointing. Somehow, he was never again able to take her to the heights of ecstasy they had scaled on the night of their first date.

Chapter 7 - **Naming the Day**

*The Gal Liza was hard to please when it came to choosing a
hat for her daughter Jemima's wedding.*

Despite the excitement of Young Jimma's wedding, when she had been
a bridesmaid, Jemima showed very little interest in following her brother
into the joyful estate of marriage.

She had seen how exasperated her mother got with her father, and
could not really understand why women got themselves caught up in these
strange relationships.

Too often she had heard her mother exclaim: "Men!" when either Ow
Jimma or Young Jimma had done something daft. And as for sex; well
Jimma and the Gal Liza had been no more explicit than their parents had
been in giving instruction on the more physical aspects of human
relationships.

And we are still talking of a time before human biology became a regular
subject on the school curriculum. To say that Jemima was innocent is to
under-state the purity of her honest mind.

Ow Jimma was discussing the problem one day with Wally Hogg. They were leaning on the rails of a pig pen at the saleyard and Jimma recalled that it was in just such a situation, whilst watching Wally's boar making amorous advances to his sow, that Wally had advised him of some of the basic techniques of human reproduction.

Indirectly, this instruction had inspired Ow Jimma and the Gal Liza to start their own family.

Wally and his wife Sarah, who had produced eight offspring, were, after all, authorities on the subject.

They had only stopped reproducing after Wally suffered a sore throat and Sarah made an appointment for him to visit the cottage hospital in the nearby town.

With the ready co-operation of her family doctor, who was fed up with being called out in the middle of the night to another confinement at the Hogg household, Wally had been anaesthetised and had slipped into unconsciousness believing he was about to have his tonsils out.

The actual operation that took place, commonly known as the "little snip", left Wally unscathed but experiencing some pain in a most unexpected place.

Assured that this was a side effect of the particularly deep rooted form of tonsilitis from which he had been suffering, Wally ever thereafter praised modern medical techniques to the skies. "Thass marvellous what they can dew nowadays," he told everybody. "I allus thought tonsils were somewhere near yer troot but I never hed a bit o' pain there!"

His sexual activities continued unabated, and if he was surprised that there were no further additions to his family, he never said so.

Now, as he and Ow Jimma stood weighing up this pen full of pigs, and trying to decide whether or not they were worth buying, Jimma remarked: "Wally, ow partner, yew once helped me out with a little parsonal problem I hed, an I're never forgot that. Trouble is, I're got another one.

"My daughter Jemima don't show no interest in boys. Dew she dorn't look sharp she'll end up a ow mearde. I wouldn't like thet ter happen 'cos I arnt a-gorn ter be around fer ever ter look arter har."

"Dew yer think there's a boy in yar large family what might like ter tearke har orf the shelf?"

"Thass a rummun yew shud say that," replied Wally. "I think I're got jist the one. He's a soppy tule an' we're bin a tryin' ter git rid on 'im fer years, but I reckon he'd suit yar Jemima a treat. His name's Arnie. Why dornt yew an' the gal Liza bring the gal Jemima round ter see 'im."

Next day Ow Jimma and the Gal Liza arrived at Wally's house with Jemima. Wally had not been exaggerating Arnie's intellect or conversational skills.

45

While Sarah fussed around getting the tea the rest of the company sat staring awkwardly at each other, nobody knowing what to say, until Wally finally broke the silence.

"Well go on!" he said, nudging Arnie in the ribs. "Say suffin to her. Jist like I towd yer ter dew."

Arnie cleared his throat awkwardly. Then, reading slowly and laboriously from a list of questions his father had written down, he recited: "How owd are yer? Can yew cook? Are yar teeth orl yar own? An' dew yew suffer from any con-tage-ous diseases - apart from yar squint?"

More silence followed. Jemima looked tentatively at her father. "I don't know what ter say," she stuttered nervously. "Jist tell the boy yew're sound in wind an' limb an' yew can cook a good apple pie," advised Ow Jimma paternally. "Thass orl he need ter know."

"Dew that mean we're engearged then?" inquired Arnie. "Blast bor, howd yew hard!" exclaimed Wally. "Yew're a-gittin ahid o' yarself. Yew're gotta walk out with the mawther fust."

So it was agreed that the two should be allowed two free hours the next evening to "walk out" with each other. "Yew cud dew wuss than hang around the chachyard wall," said Ow Jimma. "Thass where Liza an' me dun orl our courtin'."

So Arnie came calling for Jemima the following evening. When he brought her back a couple of hours later Jemima was, if possible, even more nervous than usual.

She made excuses and hurried upstairs to her bedroom. Pouring some water from the jug into the bowl on the washstand she vigorously brushed her teeth. "What is that gal up tew?" asked Ow Jimma's mother, who always came round from next-door at this time of day. The sound of gargling could be heard upstairs.

"I'll hatta go up an' see if she's orl right," said Mother, heaving herself up the narrow stairway.

Jemima was a timid soul, but if there was one person in whom she normally felt able to confide it was her grandmother. "Whass up?" inquired the old lady.

Jemima burst into tears. "Oh Granma, I'm in trouble," she sobbed. "I think I could be in the family way."

"What'd yew say?" asked the old lady, who was becoming a trifle hard of hearing in her old age. Cupping her hand round her ear she leaned forward.

"I said I think I could be in the family way," sobbed Jemima a little more loudly - but not loud enough for her parents to hear downstairs.

"Dorn't yew bother about thet," said her grandmother. "I'm in everybodda's way an' that don't bother me!"

"No, yew dunt unnerstand," cried Jemima. "I could be a-gorn ter hev a bearby. Yew see, Arnie kissed me time we wus out a-walkin' ternight, an' my friend at school used ter reckon that if a boy kiss yer thass bound ter end up wi' yew hevin' a bearby!

"Oh Granma, I reckon I must be preggernunt." Jemima collapsed in a heap, her head buried in her grandmother's lap.

The old lady gently stroked the girl's hair. Then, putting her hand under Jemima's chin, she raised the girl's tear stained face and said: "Yew hent got no need ter worry, my gal. That ent the kiss what mearke yer preggernunt, thass what that lead tew. Yew're gotta long way ter go afore yew ever git preggernunt."

Thus reassured - for she always believed her grandmother's wise words - Jemima dried her eyes and was persuaded to come downstairs where Ow Jimma and the Gal Liza had been trying very hard, but not very successfully, to make polite conversation with Arnie.

The boy's face lightened up when he saw Jemima returning with the hint of a smile playing round her lips. "Are y'orlroight now?" he asked solicitously.

"S'pose so," replied Jemima. "Dew that mean we're engearged now, then?" continued Arnie. "S'pose so," repeated Jemima, a mawther of few words. "Good," said Arnie.

There was more desultory conversation about the weather and the likely yield from the sugar beet harvest before Liza said cordially to Arnie: "Yew must be a-gittin hungry. Ent that gittin near yar tea time?"

"Yis, now yew come ter mention it," said Arnie expectantly.

"Well yew better be a-gittin hoom then," said Liza. "Yar Ma'll be a-wonderin' where yew're got tew!"

Even Arnie could take a heavy hint. He said his farewells and went home, leaving Jimma and the Gal Liza to send Jemima off to bed and start making arrangements for the wedding.

Next day Ow Jimma went round to see the young vicar to arrange the date and have the banns read. "Beggin' yar pardon, Vicar, but would yew mind if I arst ow Canon Gunn ter come an' dew the sarvice. He's a bit of a ow friend, yew might say," said Jimma.

Canon Horatio Gunn, the once formidable vicar and rural dean, who had declaimed many a hellfire sermon from the pulpit of Jimma's village church, was now a very old man and living in secluded retirement on the South Coast.

Nevertheless, a spark of the old fire glimmered in his eye when he received the invitation. Yes, provided the stern and starchy Mrs Gunn could accompany him back to his old parish, and somebody could stand by to keep him awake during the service, he would be glad to officiate.

"I will go with you, my dear," promised his wife: "Provided you promise me not to indulge too freely in the Communion wine." The Canon had always enjoyed a tipple, but nowadays Mrs Gunn guarded his intake so efficiently that Communion wine was the nearest he ever got to alcohol.

Gal Liza accompanied Jemima to the "posh frock" shop in the nearby town. "What is Modom's pleasure?" inquired the assistant, attempting the kind of superior accent which she fondly believed added a touch of class to the business.

This did not come easily to her and she constantly slipped, without always realising it, into the East Anglian accent which was her birthright.

"We're got this delightful little creation in virginal white satin with a butter muslin veil. We resarve this ensemble solely for those who have lived a totally clean, pure and wholesome single life," she said.

"On the other hand, we can offer this off-white taffeta gown, trimmed with purple, for those who have had their moments, so to speak!" She allowed herself a delicate little giggle.

"I dorn't think we can tearke neither on 'em," said the Gal Liza. "One corst tew much and th'other sartinly dornt apply ter Jemima. She'll hatta mearke dew wi' whatever I can run up at hoom."

The assistant's face dropped. It seemed she was not going to make a sale. "Mind yew," continued Liza. "I're got my outfit ter think about. What ha' yer got in the way o' hats?"

The assistant, brightening up again, led Liza over to a rack containing a selection of brightly coloured headgear, all flowers and lacey veils.

Liza tried several on, looking closely at herself in the mirror and discarding each hat in turn with a look of distaste. She was not really accustomed to wearing a hat, but she understood it was the proper code of dress for a mother at her daughter's wedding.

Finally she tried on a frothy pink confection with what looked like a bunch of grapes rakishly hanging over one ear.

The assistant, trying hard to hang on to her smile, and her patience, gushed: "What a divine effect. It's definitely your colour, Modom, and your style. It makes you look 10 years younger!"

"I aren't a-gorn ter hev that one then!" declared Liza decisively, removing the hat and replacing it none too gently on the rack. "'Cos dew that mearke me look 10 yare younger time I're got it on, that'll mearke me look 10 yare older when I tearke it orf!"

With that she turned on her heel, said: "Come yew on Jemima," and marched out of the shop, closing the door firmly behind her.

The assistant, all pretence at sophistication now gone, raised two fingers at Liza's departing back and said, rather too loudly: "I hoop that rearn on the weddin' day an yar bunyans hart like hell, yew misrable ow bugger!"

Suddenly the shop door opened again. "There ent no call ter be rude!" advised Liza firmly. "I'll tell yar boss dew yew tork ter customers like that agin," she warned the surprised and embarrassed assistant.

As the two women walked away from the shop Jemima asked her mother: "How'd yew know she'd said suffin rude?"

"I din't know," admitted Liza. "I jist guessed. I'd ha' bin rude if I'd ha' hatta deal wi' a customer like me!"

Chapter 8 -

The Omens are Not Good

Mother, pictured at her cottage door, had been a formidable, though sometimes helpful, neighbour.

The night before his wedding Arnie told his parents he was going for a walk to "clear his head." This could not have been further from the truth.

He headed straight for the Spoon and Spigot where a group of his brothers and sisters, and some of their friends, were waiting to "toast" the bridegroom.

On an impulse, he decided to take a short cut through the churchyard. As he walked along the path he caught sight of a figure lying prostrate on one of the tombstones.

At first he thought it was a stone angel, until he realised that the figure was in a far from angelic pose, and it was actually moving.

Perhaps this was a drunk, thought Arnie. Or somebody who was overcome with grief. Either way, he might be in need of help, and Arnie was a kind hearted boy.

As he approached a low moan escaped from the mournful figure. "Why did yew hatta die?" it sobbed. "Why did yew hatta die?"

Arnie took pity, and bending over the man, laid a hand on his shoulder. "Is that the grearve of yar beloved missus?" he asked kindly.

"No," said the man, turning round to reveal the most pitiful of tear stained faces. "Thass har fust husband a-lyin' in thare!"

"So why are yew a-howlin' like that?" asked the puzzled Arnie. "Blast boy, yew can tell yew arnt married," said the man. "Dew that silly bugger hent ha' parssed away like he did I wouldn't ha' finished up a-marryin' his widder.

"Blast me if that ent the warst day's wark I ever dun. She're gotta tongue on har what'd lash a carthorse inter a gallup. I reckon the only reason he pegged out was ter git away from har. Yew tearke my advice," the man continued as he stood up and steadied himself against a gravestone. "Dew yew ever git tempted to git married jist yew tearke a look at the gal's mother an' yew'll see what she's a-gorn ter grow up intew."

"That might help yew ter mearke up yar mind whether yew wanta spend the rest o' yar life wi' suffin like that. Me, I'm a-gorn ter bugger orf as sune as I git the charnce - jist like he did." He pointed at the grave.

Arnie thought of Jemima, and then he thought of Liza - and he concluded that, on the whole, the man's advice was sound. Anyway, nobody would describe this strange encounter in the churchyard as a good omen for a happy marriage.

But the appearance, at that moment, of a noisy company of young revellers reminded him that he had almost reached the point of no return.

His brothers and sisters, with their wives and girlfiends, had grown tired of waiting for Arnie in the pub and had come out to find him. "Come yew on tergather," urged his brother Tom. "We're a-gorn ter git yew plarstered for what could be the larst time in yar miserable life."

The Spoon and Spigot enjoyed one of its best nights for years. It was almost like old times as the company got noisier and noisier, and the songs became more and more raucous, out of tune and crude.

Sitting in the corner with a half-pint of beer, an old man called Huby thought of the nights he had enjoyed in this very room when the Yanks had been here during the war, and the tall stories he had told them - and they had believed - of ghostly monks and an ancient tunnel leading between the pub and the church.

There was still life and mischief in the old man. He looked out of the window and saw the reflection of a full moon in the village pond. He'd play a little game with these rowdy youngsters. Arnie would remember his stag night.

Huby turned to the barmaid and asked: "Hev yew gotta white sheet an' a hammer and chisel I could borrer?"

"Whadda yer want it for?" she asked, a trifle aggressively. "Jist ter play a little spooky jook," said Huby. "I promise yew'll git 'em back now shortly."

Huby did not drink a lot, but at least he patronised the pub every night. So the barmaid spoke to the manager. The manager moved along the bar and inclined an ear for Huby's whispered explanation.

"OK," he said. "But mind yew dornt scare 'em ter death. We need hard drinking customers like them."

It had been a good night in the pub and the manager had enjoyed "one or two" with the young revellers. So he was in a mellow mood.

Huby quietly slipped out of the pub, collected the sheet, the hammer and the chisel, and disappeared into the night.

Sometime later the stag night party spilled out of the Spoon and Spigot, singing, shouting and supporting Arnie between two muscular figures who were only marginally less incapable than he was.

"Thare's an old strill by the meam, Dellie Nean," sang Arnie loudly, inaccurately and untunefully. "Where I used ter set an' dream, Dellie Nean."

He dissolved into inane laughter. "I'm gittin' married in the mornin'," he continued loudly, showing much versatility as his family and friends propelled him towards the churchyard path and the short cut to his parents' home.

As the party moved into the churchard the laughter and song was abruptly silenced by a blood curdling shriek which echoed from the darkest recesses of the graveyard. Some said afterwards it was the most unearthly sound they had ever heard.

Huby had not exactly intended this as part of his "spooky jook". He had been waiting in the churchyard so long that he had been overcome by the demands of nature. In other words, he had been "tearken short".

He was obliged to remove his trousers, but as he bent down in the darkness his unprotected posterior descended into a clump of stinging nettles.

His shriek rent the night air. It was not part of his plan but it had the desired effect. The stag night party stopped in its tracks. Silence reigned as eyes strained in the dark direction from whence this awful cry had come.

The hoot of a barn owl heightened the air of suspense. Bats zoomed down from the belfry. "What'd yer think that wus?" whispered Tom who, being the eldest, could vaguely remember tales he had been told of Black Shuck, the devil hound of East Anglia.

Gingerly, but bravely, he stepped off the path to try and get a better look. At that moment the moon emerged from behind a cloud and a white shape was fleetingly glimpsed flitting around the gravestones and uttering incomprehensible cries.

Tom, Arnie and the rest were rooted to the spot. This must surely be the ghost of one of those old monks of whom they had heard tell. But ghosts, so they had also been told, usually walked around rattling chains and carrying their disembodied heads.

This one was holding its bottom. But then, trust this village to be different!

Suddenly they began to discern a faint, rhythmic chipping sound. They strained there ears. Yes, there it was again; chip, chip, chip; chip, chip.

A shaft of moonlight revealed the same vague white shape, now crumpled and crouched over a tombstone. Chip, chip, chip went the sound of chisel on stone.

Mournfully, a ghostly voice was moaning in the darkness. "Oh woe is me," it intoned. "Arter all what they dun ter me they went an' spelled me name wrong!" The chipping sound continued.

"Blast me," slurred Arnie, still extremely befuddled. "I see a bloke in this hare chachyard arlier on ternight what wus so unhappy about bein' married he wus a-gorn ter bugger orf. I reckon he're committed sewerside.

"I reckon his missus spelt his nearme wrong on the grearve jist ter spite 'im. Thass time I buggered orf tew - hoom!"

Arnie was far too befuddled to realise that it took more than a couple of hours to commit suicide, get buried and have a tombstone erected, albeit with one's name spelled wrongly.

Arnie lived by the maxim that discretion was the better part of valour. When you think you might be in the presence of the supernatural the best thing to do is run.

Which is exactly what Arnie did, followed by the thundering feet of the rest of his stag night friends.

His head was far from clear when he got home after his "walk". It was even less clear the following morning, despite the fact that he had snored his way through a spectacular thunderstorm.

Meanwhile, over at the home of Ow Jimma and the Gal Liza, Jemima, in her nervous state of mind, believed the thunderstorm to be a bad omen for the future.

She crept into her parents' bedroom. Gal Liza stirred and looked sleepily at her daughter. Ever since she had been a tiny girl Jemima had been frightened of thunderstorms and had sought comfort with her mother.

Gal Liza did not entirely approve of this "namby pamby" habit, as she called it.

After all, the girl never knocked and even though there was never very much activity from Jimma's side of the bed - an atom bomb wouldn't have wakened him - it was just possible that she might stumble on an embarrassing moment in their married lives. But only just possible.

Here was Jemima, about to get married, and although the young couple were only going to live next-door, a husband might not take too kindly to his wife disappearing into her parents' bedroom every time there was a storm.

It had been agreed that Jemima and Arnie would move into Mother's cottage so that the old lady could live with Jimma and Liza. More precisely, this had been decided by Mother and agreed to by Jimma, who never contradicted her. Nobody else had a say in the matter.

"I need a bit o' lookin' arter in my owd earge," Mother had declared emphatically.

Gal Liza spent most of the morning arranging Jemima's hair and headdress and supervising her daughter as she got into the dress which Liza had "run up" out of a spare bit of curtain material.

Liza was not much of a seamstress, and try as she might, the dress still looked as if it would have been more at home on the back of a coal lorry than on Jemima. It fitted where it touched.

The veil was created from a piece of muslin which Liza had last used to cook dumplings. "Well hew's a-gorn ter know no diffrent?" she retorted when Jimma asked her about her choice of material. "I mearde sure I washed it arter I cooked the dinner!"

Jimma and Liza were so keen to get their daughter safely married that the bride arrived at the church before the 'groom and had to wait.

Arnie was still at home, his head being held under the pump in the back yard by his brother Tom. "We're gotta git yew sobered up an' orf tew chach dew otherwise we'll never be rid on yer," Tom said encouragingly as he pumped the handle. The rest of his brothers dried off the spluttering Arnie, threw him into his Sunday suit and hussled him down to the church.

Ow Jimma, Young Jimma and Wally were wiling away the time playing cards in the church porch while Liza and Sarah tried hard to comfort the sniffling Jemima. "He int a-comin'," wailed the bride. "He're got cowd feet."

"That int cowd feet what he're got," said Wally. "Thass more like a sore hid! Dunt yew worry gal, his brothers'll git 'im hare."

Old Canon Gunn was quite happy about the delay. While Mrs Gunn marched up and down the church ordering all the guests to stay calm, he was comfortably ensconced in the vestry helping himself to medicinal doses of Communion wine.

By the time Arnie was dragged into church, hanging limply between two of his brothers, Mrs Gunn was wearing her fiercest glare and Jemima was a bag of nerves.

"The Canon's wife banged on the vestry door. "Come along Horatio," she commanded. "It's time to start!"

Nothing happened. Except that the sound of a snore issued from the other side of the vestry door.

The organ was playing Here Comes the Bride as Jemima walked up the aisle on Ow Jimma's arm and stood beside Arnie, who was leaning heavily on Tom, his best man.

"Horatio!" shouted Mrs Gunn. The vestry door opened and Canon Gunn stood there, rubbing his eyes. "Ish it time to start?" he asked, a loud hiccup destroying his feeble attempt at clerical dignity.

He walked unsteadily across the chancel and stood swaying before the happy couple. "Ashes to ashes; dust to dust," he recited, hiccupping again. "We came into thish warld with nothing and. . . . ." his voice trailed away as his wife hissed: "You've got the wrong service!"

Covered with embarrassment, she took his prayer book and found the right page. Considering all things the service went well, the Canon constantly being prompted by his wife, and Arnie, who was asleep on his feet, being heavily nudged by Tom when it was time for him to speak up.

At the end of the ceremony, as the happy couple were signing the register, Ow Jimma suddenly remembered that it was the job of the bride's father to pay the bill for the church.

"How much dew I owe yer?" he asked the Canon. "How much do you think she's worth?" returned the old man, still somewhat under the influence.

Jimma looked his daughter up and down, assessed the overall effect of the gown Liza had made, put his hand in his pocket and drew out a ten shilling note (50p).

"That's very generous of you," remarked the Canon appreciatively. Standing back, he also took a long look at the happy bride. Then he put his hand in his pocket and took out five shillings (25p). "Here's your change!" he said, handing it to Jimma.

The company repaired to the restaurant at the Spoon and Spigot where everybody enjoyed a sit-down meal of ham salad. Everybody, that is, except Huby. Much to the puzzlement, and amusement, of the other guests, he inexplicably remained standing throughout, declining several offers of a chair.

Arnie and Jemima left for their honeymoon amid a storm of confetti and gales of laughter sparked by shafts of crude wit.

They were only going to their cottage for their wedding night but the unitiated observer might have thought, from the send-off, that they were heading for the ends of the earth.

Wally Hogg turned to Sarah and said, with a sigh of relief: "Well, at least we're got 'im orf our hands. I wus really startin' ter think he wus one o' them sort what hang around at hoom fer ever."

His optimism was short lived. Later that night, as Wally and Sarah were thinking about going to bed, the back door opened and in walked Arnie.

"What're yew a-dewin' on back hoom hare this sune?" demanded Wally. "Yew shud be orl tucked up nicely an' gittin yar oots by now, boy."

Arnie turned to his mother and explained. "When I went up ter the bedrume Jemima wus orlreddy in bed. She wus a-snifflin' a bit an' I arst her why. She say: 'I hent never dun this afore.' So I come hoom."

"Yew dun right boy," said Sarah soothingly. "Dew she int good enough fer th'other boys in the village she int good enough fer yew!"

Wally was not so sympathetic. Next morning he took Arnie by the scruff of his neck and marched him back to the still sniffling Jemima.

"Yew tew ha' married each other fer better or wass," he declared. "Yew probly think married life may be more wass than better - which, knowin' yew tew, I dornt doubt yew may be right. But yew're mearde yar bed an' yew're jist gotta lay onnit." It was, indeed, an unpromising start to wedded bliss.

The ceremony left a small mystery unsolved. "I wonder why that hammer an' chisel tarned up in the chachyard the day o' yar dorter's weddin'," said the churchwarden to Ow Jimma.

"That might ha' bin a hint from Him Up There that we orta be a-startin' ter dew our chach up a bit. That dew begin ter look a bit the wass fer wear. Anyway, I're put 'em in me tool box - just in cearse we need 'em."

Meanwhile, over at the Spoon and Spigot, Huby, having searched the churchyard in vain, was apologising to the manager. "I'll hatta buy yer some new ones next time I go ter town," he said.

He was beginning to wonder why he had bothered with his "spooky jook".

Chapter 9 - **Keeping the Faith**

It was a hot day when Ow Jimma and Arnie, his new son-in-law, dug the garden of the young couple's cottage. Gal Liza reckoned they looked "sorft" with their knotted handkerchiefs on their heads

The faithful service offered by Ow Jimma's family to the village church had gone back generations. Jimma himself had inherited his father's seat next to the Vicar's, and with it his place in the choir.

However, the regularity of his attendance at church had become something of an embarrassment to the young vicar.

Jimma had always sung the hymns and psalms with great gusto. In fact, as he grew older his voice seemed to grow louder, even in the passages which were supposed to be quiet. It had also, unfortunately, grown less tuneful.

One day the Vicar, whose seat was so close to Jimma that he had begun to worry about the danger of going deaf in one ear, felt the time had come to do something about the problem.

"I don't want to offend people who have been such faithful servants of the Church as Jimma has," he confided to the churchwarden. "But I really believe we shall have to find some way of easing him out of the choir.

"His singing is not only making it difficult to recruit other choristers, but it is also discouraging people from coming to church at all.

"However, in view of his long and faithful service we shall have to approach this problem with the utmost diplomacy."

"Leave that ter me," said the churchwarden. "Yew want diplomacy; yew'll git diplomacy. I'll jist tell the ow bugger we dunt want 'im in the choir no more, beggin' yer pardon!"

"Oh, please don't do that," exclaimed the Vicar hurriedly. "We don't want to lose him altogether. After all, his wife and mother help with the Mothers' Union and we might lose them as well. Find him another little job in the church."

"Well," said the churchwarden, rubbing his chin thoughtfully: "We could dew with a varger. We're got what yer might call a vearcancy there an' I reckon ow Jimma could dew thet thare job roight noicely."

The churchwarden had held his important appointment for years. He had dealt with tricky situations like this before. So he had a quiet word with Jimma.

"Yew see, ow partner, thass loike this hare," he said conspiratorially. "We're bin without a varger fer some toime an' the Vicar he're bin down on his knees a'prayin' fer a volunteer.

"He reckon th'other noight, jist as he wus at his wits' end a-wonderin' what ter dew, he see a blindin' white light an' hard a greart thunderin' voice a sayin': 'Dew yew gorn arst the Boy Jimma. He's the man fer the job.'

"So the Vicar reckon that musta bin Him Up Thare what ha' fingered yew. I reckon dew yew went along ter the Vicar an offered yar sarvices he'd think his prayers hed bin arnswered an' that'd mearke sure o' yar plearce in Heaven!"

"But I like a-singin' in the choir!" protested Jimma. "I know thet," retorted the churchwarden. "But jist yew remember, that ent what yew want, thass what God want wass important. He chose yew ter be varger an' yew orta feel greartly 'onnered."

Jimma was a simple soul, which was why he had qualified as the official village idiot. He approached the Vicar.

That cleric was hard pressed to stifle an expression of amazement when Jimma said, in his humblest voice and with eyes cast piously heavenwards: "I hare yew wanta varger. I'd be pleased ter dew the job dew yew think I'm up ter it, an' yew think yew can manage wi'out me in the choir."

It was hard to tell whether Jimma was talking to the Vicar or addressing his offer directly to "Him Up Thare". The Vicar accepted Jimma's offer with alacrity, assuring him that, much as his presence would be missed in the choir, the other singers would struggle on manfully.

That night he really was on his knees. "I don't know how you did it, Lord," he prayed in gratitude. "But You certainly do work in most mysterious ways, Your wonders to perform!"

For a time everybody was happy. Jimma took to his new job with enthusiasm. In fact, he rapidly became rather bossy.

When visitors came to his church he would conduct them round the building with great solemnity, pointing out its architectural features and memorials, and then standing by the door as they left, shaking a collection plate meaningfully at them.

The income of the church began to rise noticeably. As time went on Ow Jimma, now becoming accustomed to meeting all these "furriners", grew bolder.

One day a coachload of visitors from another village, who had been on a "mystery tour" organised by their local squire, was shown round the church with all due formality.

As they left Jimma stood by the door and held the plate, muttering "Thankyer very koindly," every time a coin chinked into it. The squire, a large red faced man with handlebar moustache, Norfolk jacket, plus fours and a military bearing, passed without so much as a glance at Jimma.

The party moved down the church path and were just boarding their coach, the squire bringing up the rear, when there came the sound of Jimma's boots crunching along the path, and the rattle of coins in a plate.

He approached the squire. "H'excuse me, Yar Warship," he said respectfully. "I'm oonly a-tryin' ter be helpful, yew unnerstand, but dew yew git hoom an' find yew're lorst yar wallet, jist yew remember yew din't git that out hare!"

He held the plate in the squire's direction. That distinguished figure, even more red faced than ever, looked at his sniggering followers, felt in his trousers pocket and drew out a coin.

Folding his huge hand around it so that it was impossible for anybody to detect its value, he surreptciously placed it in the plate, attempting to hide it under the others that were already there.

The coach completed loading and as the squire sat down Jimma climbed on board. "Out o' respec fer yar squire," he announced loudly. "I jist wanted yew orl ter know that he can rest easy he're dun the roight thing. Arter orl, a threepenny bit IS better'n any other coin on account o' thet go ter chach most often!"

Catching sight of the expression on the face of the glowering squire, he added: "Orl roight, I'm a-gorn!" and got off the bus.

The Mother's Union met once a week on a Wednesday afternoon. A great deal of work was done for the church but there was always an interval for a cup of tea and a home-made Suffolk rusk.

Mother enjoyed the refreshment time. She loved baking cakes and always took one to the meeting in the knowledge that it would inspire plenty of compliments from her appreciative friends.

Cup-of-tea time was also the opportunity for a good gossip; a time to catch up on the village news and to swop rumours, opinions and personal views.

"Hev yew read the local pearper this week?" Sarah asked Mother one Wednesday afternoon. "That say the cownsil is thinkin' about drivin' a new roadway through the chachyard an' distarbin' a lotta grearves."

"My hart alive!" observed Mother. "I dornt howd wi' that idea; especially arter orl them people thort they wus a-gorn ter be in thare fer the rest o' their loives!

"Anyway," she added: "My ow boy's in thare an" I know he'll hev suffin ter say about that."

Sarah changed the subject. She obviously was not going to make much progress discussing new roads through churchyards.

"I went ter King's Lynn on the bus larst week ter dew some shoppin'," she reported. "My Wally hed arst me ter gorn buy him some red an' white spotted paint an' a bag o' rubber tin tacks.

"That wus his idea of a jook," she added unnecessarily. "Even arter we're bin tergather orl these years he still think I'm sorft."

"Anyway, the ironmongers wus sellin' them new type o' toilet brushes wi' the stiff bristles so I bought tew on 'em."

"Oh ah," said Mother. "How are yer gittin' on with 'em?"

"Well, I keep a parseverin'," replied Sarah. "But my Wally ha' give up on 'em an' gone back ter usin' pearper!

"He reckon he couldn't nicely sit down ter eat his dinner without a-jifflin' about. That mearde him hully bad tempered an orl!"

"Well that sarve yer roight," said Mother unsympathetically. "Yew shouldn't be allus wantin' to try out new ideas. The old ways are still the best."

The following week the Mother's Union welcomed a special guest speaker. Farmer Greengrass's sister-in-law was paying one of her mercifully infrequent visits to the village from her home in London.

Farmer Greengrass was pleased that her visits were infrequent because, having once been jilted by a young farmer 40 years before, she had since maintained firm and sharply critical opinions of men in general and farmers in particular. She had a habit of expressing these opinions at considerable length.

"She allus come fer a week an' stay a month," Farmer Greengrass had once remarked to Ow Jimma. "Blast me if she int so narrer minded she can see through a keyhole with booth eyes at once!"

Farmer Greengrass's sister-in-law had been invited to speak to the Mother's Union on condition she kept off the subject of men. So she decided to tell her country cousins about "My life in the big city."

During the tea interval she found herself talking to Mother, and realised that she had not seen the old lady since the death of Jimma's father.

"Even though I don't like men, and never did care for your husband very much," she said honestly. "I was sorry to hear that he had died and left you all alone. Was it sudden?"

Mother considered the question. She had very little time for Farmer Greengrass's sister-in-law whom she regarded as "one o' them city fook what think us country people are darft." Here might be a chance to prove the old so-and-so wrong.

"I s'pose yew might call that sudden," she said. "That happened one Sunday mornin'. I got up an' he said he wus a-gorn ter hev a little lay in. I called him agin at nine o-clock an' he said he'd be down in a little while, but he still weren't down at half parst.

"So I went upstairs, an' dew yew know what?" she continued, pausing for maximum dramatic effect. "There he wus slumped back in the bed an' out like a light. I dorn't know whether he'd gorn upstairs or downstairs!"

"Oh dear," said the visitor, with uncharacteristic sympathy. "It must have been a terrible shock."

"Well, thet sartinly musta bin fer 'im," agreed Mother. "Mind yew, that wus orl his own fault 'cos dew he'd ha got up when I towd 'im tew he mighta bin alive terday!"

Farmer Greengrass's sister-in-law was not entirely certain whether to remain sympathetic or give way to her vaguely annoying suspicion that the old lady might just have been having a macabre joke at her expense.

But she persevered. In a more practical and down-to-earth tone she inquired: "Did your dear departed husband leave much money?"

"What are yew a-gittin' at?" exclaimed the old lady scornfully. "He left all onnit, o' course. Yew're got tew!"

"If he wus nothin' else, at least he wus honest," she added with dignity.

"Peasants!" thought Farmer Greengrass's sister-in-law next day as she boarded the train for London. "I'll be glad to get back to civilisation."

"Blast I'm glad she's gorn," thought Farmer Greengrass as he and his wife, smiling and waving at their departing guest, disappeared in the cloud of steam which issued from the train as it huffed out of the station. "Now we can git back ter livin' like civilised country people."

Chapter 10 -
The Reunion

*Jimma's long association
with the village church
went back to his days as
a choirboy. Years later, as
his singing became
charged with enthusiasm
rather than melody, he
was "called" to a new
mission in life as verger.*

Jimma's friend Huby -
he who had sustained
nettle rash around his
nether regions on the
night of Arnie's stag party
- was a porter at the village
railway station.

By nature a quiet and
introspective man - not to
say dour - he had blossomed into a rural raconteur during the war, inspired
by the American GIs who, based at the nearby airfield, had proved an
eager and gullible audience during his nightly story telling sessions at the
old Pig and Whistle.

In fact, the arrival of the Americans had caused such a transformation
in Huby that for the rest of his life he was seen in the village as a man of
lively and inventive wit. The dramatic change was as a humble caterpillar
turns into a lustrous butterfly.

Huby would spin many a yarn about Victorian train crashes, smugglers
bringing contraband up the river and hiding it in the village church whose
ornate roof, covered in carved angels, still bore the scars inflicted by musket
balls fired at it by Cromwellian troops.

He would tell of Black Shuck, the East Anglian hell hound which had
terrorised whole communities in the dark ages, and whose ghostly apparition
still stalked the village on moonless nights.

And he would speak of the mediaeval monks, who had smuggled ale and other commodities along a tunnel between church and pub, with a familiarity which had almost suggested that he knew them personally.

Huby had encouraged his wife to accompany him on these nightly visits to the pub after discovering that, while he had been entertaining the troops in the tap room, she had been offering them more intimate diversions at home.

His initial distress at this discovery was tempered by the fact that the GIs not only showered gifts on his missus but also plundered their food stores to provide provisions which handsomely supplemented the family's meagre postwar rations.

After the war, some of the lustre of Huby's tale telling talent wore off. He and his wife continued to inhabit the railway cottages, where he retreated back into his shell and adopted his natural lugubrious demeanour. But there were occasions when flashes of the old wartime spirit surfaced, as on the aforementioned stag night.

However, the real revival of Huby the Teller of Tall Tales came when a group of Americans returned to their wartime stamping ground for a nostalgic reunion.

The serious reason for their return was to dedicate a stained glass window which had been installed in the village church as a memorial to their comrades in arms who had made the ultimate sacrifice for freedom. It was to be an emotional occasion. But it would also leave time for many parties - and for Jimma and Huby to remind the visitors of the days when, as brash and confident young soldiers, they had boasted that everything in "The States" was bigger and better than in the tiny island to which they had been sent.

Huby's working day was divided into a succession of brief peaks of activity. These occurred whenever a train arrived. There were about eight each day (four in each direction), and each arrival would find him marching up and down the platform, carrying luggage to the guard's van and bawling the name of the station at the top of his voice.

When all the passengers had either boarded or alighted from the train there would be much slamming of doors and Huby would call: "Right away Charlie," to the guard. With a wave of Charlie's flag, and an eruption of steam, the train would depart and Huby would return to work.

His habit was to occupy the intervals between trains either chatting to the signalman in the signal box, cleaning the brasses in the "Gentlemen's" - to preserve a sense of decency his wife came in to clean the "Ladies" - or tending the vegetables on his lineside allotment garden.

Station staff had turned some of the land beside the track into productive plots, and the sale of produce to villagers and passengers provided a useful means of supplementing their modest incomes.

The highlight of each working day at the station was the moment when the "up express" thundered through. It was the one direct train for London which travelled along this modest line, and it never stopped at such insignificant stations as Huby's.

In typically English fashion a committee had been formed in the village to organise a welcome party for the Americans at the village hall. They were due to arrive by train - just as they had during the war.

Ow Jimma was picked to meet them at the main line station and accompany them along the branch line which, in those days, still linked their village to the national rail network.

It was a major adventure for Jimma who had not been further than the nearest market town since spending an unsatisfactory honeymoon in Lowestoft many years before.

As soon as the excited ex-GIs saw him waiting on the platform they surrounded him with noisy good humour. "Gee, it's great to be back," they exclaimed as one man, slapping him on the back so hard his false teeth shot out of his mouth and landed perilously close to the edge of the platform.

He retrieved them sheepishly, just as the branch line train chugged into the station. Forewarned that there would be an unusually large number of passengers that day, the railway authorities had put on a couple of extra coaches and supplied two ancient engines, their tall funnels belching black smoke. The train set off and ground round the bend on to the village line. There was hardly time for it to pick up speed before it had to slow down again. It was passing a signal box where the driver had to collect a staff which ensured that only one train was on the single track branch at a time.

As the train trundled onwards, stopping at each trackside halt, one of the visitors remarked conversationally: "Gee, your trains are slow."

"Still," he added with a mischievous twinkle in his eye: "I reckon they have to be, 'cos this 'ere island of yours is so small that if'n they went any faster they'd fall off the edge!"

He sat back to observe the effect of his wit on Jimma, who was looking out of the window. "Dun't yew judge orl our trearns by this 'un," said Jimma. "Thass only a stopper."

Still looking out of the window, he added: "They tell me we're got some expresses what are so fast yew carn't see outa the winder fer telegraph pools!"

The American was still pondering the point of this remark when the train pulled into Jimma's village station. "Ah think Ah recognarse that voice," said the leader of the American party as Huby's stentorian bellow was heard echoing up and down the platform.

The Americans spilled off the train and subjected Huby to an even more boisterous greeting than that which they had inflicted on Jimma.

"Ah know this man," said the American leader, a large man called Gus. He wore a brightly coloured sheepskin coat and a bright blue baseball cap. He also had a huge cigar apparently stuck permanently to his lips.

"You-all remember Black Shuck and all them ghostly monks?" he asked his fellow visitors. "Gee, what nights we had in that little ole pub!"

Huby was gratified that they had not forgotten. But the expression "little ole pub" reminded both Huby and Jimma of the days when the Americans had applied it to just about everything English.

At that moment there was a faint rumble in the distance. The Americans paused. "Is it going to rain?" asked Gus, remembering all those dark, wet and windy wartime nights which had convinced him that Noah had been an Englishman.

Huby knew that the "up express" was due. But he said nothing. The "stopper" train had been shunted into a siding. The rumble grew into a hissing, panting, rushing sound as the express roared round the bend and thundered through the station.

A monster engine followed by 11 coaches thundered past - thickety-thack, thickety-thack. The sound was deafening. All conversation was impossible.

As the train disappeared into the distance Gus recovered his voice. "What was that?" he asked. "What was what?" returned Huby, innocently looking round him as if nothing had happened.

"That train," returned Gus. "What train?" asked Huby maddeningly.

"The one that just hurtled through the station!" said Gus, his patience beginning to run out.

"Oh that," remarked Huby, as straight faced as ever. "That wunt no train; that wus oonly ow Billy a-pushin' a few cooches inter the shuntin' yard!"

By now Gus realised that he was the victim of a gentle East Anglian leg pull. "Nuthin's changed in this 'ere God-forsaken part of the world, I see," he remarked. But the smile on his face and the glint in his eye betrayed the affection with which he said it.

Changing the subject, he pointed in the direction of Huby's garden and said: "I'm puzzled by the crops you're growing there. Can you tell me what they are, Bud? What are them red things with green tops."

"Blast," said Huby; "Yew Yanks dunt' seem ter know much; they're carrots."

"Carrots?" responded Gus, surprised. "Back home in the State of Texas we have carrots many times bigger than them li'l things. What are those round green things?"

"Blast bor, they're cabbages," said Huby. "Hen't yew never sin none o' them afore?"

"Cabbages? Our cabbages are durn grit things, bigger'n your pumpkins," replied the Texan. "What're them li'l green things on storks?"

"Them?" said Huby. "Moi hart aloive, they're Brussel sprouts. Dun't tell me yew hen't never sin them afore?" "Yes sirree, but in Texas Brussel sprouts are about the size of your cabbages," said Gus.

"Oh ah," said Huby, bending down to pick out a weed from between the rows. And that was all he said.

It was Jimma's turn to take charge. "Praps dew yew foller me, we can tearke a little walk thru the village an' yew can hev a little look round afore the offishul ceremonies start," he said.

The group walked through the village, Jimma pointing out various landmarks as they went. Rounding a corner they came upon the gasworks. Two large round gas holders rose towards the cloudy sky, a flight of steps leading up one side.

"What are those things?" asked Gus. "I'm surprised yew hen't sin them afore," replied Jimma, helpfully: "They're the saucepans we bile yar American sprouts in!"

"I suppose I deserved that," admitted Gus. But he didn't learn his lesson.

Walking on through the village they saw, at the end of its long drive, the "big house", formerly the ancient seat of Lord and Lady Wymond-Hayme.

"Whaddaya think o' that plearce," said Jimma. "Thass hully historic. That wus built in the rayn o' the fust Queen Elizabeth an' thatta got 32 bedrumes, at least two bathrumes an' a inside privy. That took twetty-odd yare ter build that."

"Historic it might be," said the GI: "But we could have built one in half the time in the States."

In the centre of the village they came to the church, a building with which Jimma was all too familiar. He resisted the temptation to go inside and fetch the collection plate. He knew his opportunity would come before the generous Americans went home.

"En't that bewtiful?" said Jimma. "Thass hundreds o' yare owd; the walls a six-feet thick and that took thatty-odd yare ter build that."

"It's certainly old, I'll give you that," acknowledged Gus. "But we could have built one in half the time in the States."

Further on they came to the new secondary modern school. Built since the war it was the most modern building in the village and the elements had not yet rubbed the shine off the brickwork.

"What's that place?" inquired the Texan. By this time Jimma was exasperated by hearing how much quicker the Americans were at building historic monuments. "I dun't roightly know," he replied, scratching his head and adopting a puzzled expression; "That wun't there this mornin'!"

Later the party returned to the church. Villagers and visitors joined in a moving service to dedicate the memorial. Old friendships were renewed, tears flowed.

East Anglians suffer a largely undeserved reputation for being dour and uncommunicative, unable or unwilling to throw open their homes and hearts to visitors.

The returning Americans already knew this was untrue. And the welcome which awaited them at the village hall that evening overwhelmed them with warmth.

Bunting bedecked the room and the trestle tables groaned under the weight of home made pies, cakes, scones, rusks and sausage rolls.

"We'll certainly be back," said Gus, beaming at Jimma, Liza, Huby, Wally, Sarah and the rest of the villagers as the band launched into a passable rendition of "String of Pearls". He added: "I wouldn't have missed the war for anything. I gave me the chance to meet you wonderful people."

There were many memories to be revived. After hostilities had ceased and the GIs had gone home the village had returned to a peacefully gentle pace of life. But the Yanks had left their mark.

The derelict hangars, barrack huts, canteens and control towers on the old camp, which had once been filled with the shouts of men at work, the roar of aircraft engines and the music of Glenn Miller, now echoed emptily to the voices of exploring village children.

Wildlife and undergrowth reclaimed some of them while others were put to good use by farmers and light engineering businesses.

Some of the control towers and Nissen huts were turned into museums in tribute to the Americans who had come from a land of bright lights and bounty to a benighted and blacked out wilderness, had found friends and had given their lives for a freedom which they had not realised was under threat.

The people of East Anglia never forgot their wartime guests and many are the trans-Atlantic links which exist today.

But the ghost of that wailing monk no longer calls at the village pub. Somehow the returning GIs just did not feel quite so welcome in the Spoon and Spigot as they had in the tap room of the old Pig and Whistle during the darkest days of war.

Chapter 11 - **Foreign Travels**

*A special "two header" train brought the returning GIs
back to the village for their reunion.*

"Ah sure would lark you to come over to The States," Gus said to Huby before the American visitors left.

"Blast thass roight koind on yer," enthused Huby. "But I hent never bin furrin afore. I won't know what ter dew, an' ter tell yew the trewth I ent tew well britched jist at the moment."

"Well, ah don't know about that," responded Gus, giving Huby an appraising look. "Your pants look OK to me."

"No, yew dunt unnerstand," explained Huby. Moving closer he put his hand to his mouth and his mouth close to the American's ear. "What I meant wus I hent gotta lotta money, but I dunt want everybodda ter know.

"I may not ha' bin far but I dew know the Steartes is a long way orf so I dornt doubt that corst a bob or two ter git thare."

Huby was perfectly well aware that everybody in the village knew most of everybody else's business, and it was common knowledge that railway workers were not well paid. But he was a proud man and did not want to be heard to admit to poverty.

Gus instinctively understood this. Taking Huby aside, he said quietly: "Ah'm secertary of mah veterans' association in the States, as you well know. Ah'm sure mah members would jist lurv to have you tell your stories about Black Shuck and the ghostly monks at one of our meetings.

"Mahnd you," he added as an afterthought. "I aint too sure they'll all understand everything you say.

"But we'd be glad to pay out of our association funds fer you and your wife Hannah to visit. We'll organarse fer a car to meet you at the airport and bring you to mah home where you can stay. You won't have to worry about money at all."

Gus was true to his word. A few weeks later an Airmail letter landed on Huby's doormat. It was an unusual enough occurrence for any kind of a letter to land there, so Huby held it in his hand with a sense of mounting excitement.

In fact, Huby and Hannah hadn't received a personal letter since her twin brother, Billy Dunn, who had been attracted by the bright lights of city life and had gone to live in London some years before, had written to tell them what the big city was like.

Villagers had often said that Billy was "a bit loosely put together." In fact, they had nick-named him "Under" Dunn for that reason.

Hannah was known as "Over" Dunn for reasons which few villagers ever felt the need to go into, but which may have had something to do with the war.

Billy was certainly not one for writing letters. His one and only missive had started: "Dare Huby an' Hannah, I'm a-writin' this hare letter slow on account of I know yew can't read fast."

It had ended with the following postscript. "PS: I wus a-gorn ter put a couple o' quid in fer yar Xmas presents but I'm sorry ter say I're orlreddy licked the envelope up!"

Over the years Huby and Hannah tried hard to relegate Billy to the back of their minds, and in the weeks since the visit of the Americans they had also done their best to forget the promise of a trip to "the Steartes".

"I carnt see them wantin' us over there," Huby had said several times. "Anyway, I ent tew sure I'd wanta go."

"What?" said his wife with a blank expression on her face. Huby was accustomed to this. She probably hadn't the faintest idea what he was on about.

Hannah had acquired something of a reputation for being "no better than she should be" during the war. She had taken her obligation to welcome her American allies a little too intimately to heart, some thought. And they were not too sure they believed her when she attributed this fulsome hospitality partly to the fact that she was deaf.

She claimed that, having misheard the original proposition, she had often been surprised to end up in compromising circumstances with a GI.

"I thought he said, "Shall I fetch the bread?' but he reckon he'd arst 'Shall we go ter bed?'" Hannah had explained lamely to Huby when he had come home from the pub early one night and glimpsed a burly American sergeant being hustled furtively out of the house.

"Anyway, I'd orlreddy said yis so what could I dew?" she pleaded pitifully. "I dint wanta appear unfriendly!"

Hannah was of chunky build and forbidding appearance. But the Americans, far from home, had been desperate for female company, and had introduced a level of passion into her life which she would not have believed possible.

Huby, a forgiving soul, was the only person in the village who had taken her explanation seriously enough to forgive her. They had been the subject of village gossip ever since the war, and even before the reunion Huby had thought it prudent to warn his wife: "Dunt yew go gittin tew friendly longa them Yanks agin."

"Dunt yew worry about me," she had assured him. "I ent a-gorn ter hev much opportunity 'cos they ent stayin' long enough. Anyway, some on 'em are bringin' their wives."

Hannah knew Huby would never throw her out. He was a practical man and she was a good cook. He doubted if he would ever find anybody else to feed him as well as she did.

He could put up with her little faults - even though this did mean coping with her increasing deafness.

He held the letter in his hand for a long time, turning it over, marvelling at the Texas postmark and thinking: "Blast this hare letter ha' come a helluva long way." "Shall I open it?" he asked Hannah,

"What?" she said again. Then she added: "I reckon yew better open it dew you wunt know wass inside!"

He licked his thumb carefully and inserted it in the flap. Two airline tickets fell out.

A week later a taxi arrived at No.1 Railway Cottages. A small crowd had gathered to see Huby and Hannah off, and there were many cries of "Fare yer wel tergather," and "Moind yew hev a good toime," and "Mind yew dunt come hoom a-torkin' in a fancy American voice," and "Mind yew keep yar legs crorssed Hannah.'

This last exhortation was said more quietly as the taxi passed out of earshot in the direction of the "tarnpike" which led eventually to London.

The taxi driver, having been handsomely paid by the Americans for his services, found them their flight at Heathrow Airport. Another car and driver met them at the other end.

Huby and Hannah were dazzled by America. After all this time, they began to realise that the things the GIs had said seemed to be true. Everything did seem to be bigger in "The States" than in England. Not better, necessarily, but certainly bigger.

In fact, the journey was so long from the airport to Gus's home that the driver had to stop to refuel the car.

Huby got out with him while Hannah remained in the vehicle. "What hev yew stopped hare for?" he asked. "To get some gas," explained the driver, giving Huby an "old fashioned" look.

"Gas?," said Huby, mystified. "We run our cars on petrol at hoom."

"What'd he say?" inquired Hannah from inside the car. "He reckon they run their cars on gas instead o' petrol," shouted Huby. "Ooh ah," his wife responded. "Thass a rum ow job, I must say."

"You'd better check the tyres," said the driver to the gas station attendant. "You'll find the spare in the trunk."

"I think I orta tell yer, outa fairness yew might say, that we hent brought a trunk," said Huby in the manner of someone who was humouring an idiot. "We're got orl our spare stuff in suitcearses."

The driver paused. "The trunk is at the back of the car," he said in a long suffering voice and with a pained expression on his face.

"What'd he say?" called Hannah, cupping her hand to her ear to catch Huby's reply. "He reckon they're a-gorn ter look in our suitcearses an' check our trunks," yelled her husband. "Ooh aah," she responded again, reluctant to admit that she was none the wiser.

"Whadda he think we want trunks for; we aren't a-gorn swimmin' are we? Onless thass their fancy American ward fer my bloomers? Yew better keep yar ow glimmers (eyes) open an' watch what they're a dewin on!"

"Tearke no notice o' har," said Huby apologetically to the gas station man. "In a week she's about up ter Wensdy night."

Now it was the attendant's turn to look perplexed as the driver turned to him again and said: "You might as well have a look under the hood. The weather's warm and she may need a bit of oil or water."

Huby looked at the driver in a way which made it plain that he was now convinced the man was totally "orf his hid."

"I shouldn't hatta tell yer this," he began. "But yar car hent got no hood. I think yew'll find the ceilin's made o' tin!"

The driver turned to Huby with an expression which suggested he was about to tell him to button his lip. But he thought better of it and simply said: "The hood's at the front."

"What'd he say?" called the mystified Hannah from inside the car. Lip reading was not one of her talents, especially not in American.

"He's a-gorn ter put our hood up," yelled Huby. "Blast, what the hell dew he wanta go a-dewin that for?" exclaimed Hannah. "That int rearnin' nor yit is that likely tew. Thare ent a cloud in the sky."

The gas station man was not one of nature's brightest sparks, but by this time even he had deduced that Huby and Hannah were from some strange country which was not part of the good old U.S. of A.

"Where do these two come from?" he asked. The driver raised his eyes to the heavens and said: "England, couldn't you guess?"

As the gas station man ducked his head under the bonnet to check the oil he asked Huby: "Where exactly in England do you come from, friend?"

"East Anglia," replied Huby proudly. "Gee Bud, that's a coincidence," said the attendant. "Ah flew from there durin' the war."

Drawing Huby closer he confided: "The thing ah most remember li'l ole England for is that in all mah time in the Eighth Air Force I only got laid once, and it wus the worst bit of nooky I've ever had in all ma life."

"What'd he say?" screamed Hannah from inside the car. Huby straightened up. "He reckon he knew yew durin' the war!" he yelled loudly enough for the whole neighbourhood to hear.

"Shut yew up," said Hannah. But she said it more quietly, and she did not add any further comment for fear that she might incriminate herself.

The rest of the journey was uneventful. Huby and Hannah were overwhelmed by the warmth of American hospitality. Huby's meeting with the veterans seemed to go well, and he and Hannah were invited to many parties and barbecues.

They dealt with all the questions fired at them about England as informatively and tactfully as they could, bearing in mind that they had never before travelled further from their home village than Norwich or Ipswich.

No, they were sorry, but they didn't know a Mrs Brown who lived in Birmingham, and it might be a bit difficult to call in on somebody's cousin Tex who had settled in Scotland.

But when the time came for them to leave, there were many tearful farewells. "Blast we din't harf hev a good time," Huby told Jimma the day after they got home. "Them Yanks din't harf look arter us roight nice.

"Mind yew," he added thoughtfully. "I'd ha' got on a lot better if some on 'em hadda torked proper English. I couldn't onnerstand harf o' what some on 'em said."

Meanwhile, over in Texas, the veterans gathered for their next monthly meeting. Turning to Gus, the president, a former B17 navigator, said: "Great idea of yours to get that guy over from England.

"Trouble is, I always had trouble understanding his stories during the war and I didn't do any better this time."

Which suggests that, if America and England are two nations separated by a common language, how on earth can a Texan ever be expected to understand an East Anglian - or vice versa, for that matter?

Chapter 12 -
The Second Honeymoon

Huby, the railway porter, had entertained the Americans with his wartime tales and was subsequently to enjoy their hospitality.

There came a time, as there probably does in many people's marriages, when Ow Jimma and the Gal Liza began to realise that they were taking each other for granted. "We even bought one o' them water beds but that din't stop us driftin' apart!" Jimma told Jarge one day.

"We're bin tergather now fer the best part of a tidy while, an dew yew git the feelin' that some o' the magic ha' gorn outa our marriage?" said Liza to her husband.

"Yew never wus much cop when that come ter romance," she added unsympathetically, but accurately.

"In fact, thass a wunder we ever got two kids," she added inadvisedly, before remembering that some doubt still hung over Jemima's ancestry.

"I aren't a-gorn ter say tew much about how we got two kids," said Jimma. "But I will allow that I hent 'xactly swep' yew orfa yar feet fer some time. "Mind yew," he added defensively. "I ent as bad as ow Huby is. He towd me he took Hannah ter the doctor's th'other day 'cos he reckon she's a miserable ow hin what hint never smiled since the Yanks wus here durin' the war.

"The doctor towd Huby he knew 'xacly what'd bring a smile ter har fearce, but Huby say he din't rightly unnerstand. So the doctor offered ter give a practical demonstrearshun.

"He took Hannah on his couch an' mearde mad passionate love to har, and blast if she din't smile roight bewtiful." Doctor towd Huby: 'Thare y'are; thass orl she need. About twice a week.' So Huby reckon he's a-tearkin' Hannah back ter the sargery a-Tharsdy fer another go! Thass a rummun what yew're gotta dew ter mearke some people happy!"

"Well, I reckon Huby musta bin spinnin' yew a yarn," said Liza. "I don't think Hannah'd fancy that thare doctor no more'n what I would. He deal wi' people whata got all manner o' conteargious diseases. Yew cant tell where he're bin.

"'Sides," she added. "He towd me th'other day he're bin practising in this hare village for over forty yare. I reckon dew he's still a-practising arter orl that time, an' hent got the hang onnit yit, he can't be verra quick on th'uptake!"

"But we aren't here ter talk about the doctor," she continued. "What are yew a-gorn ter dew ter put a bit more of a spark inter our marriage?" At this point it should be explained that Liza had already taken advice on how to get more romantic action out of Jimma. And that advice had come, by coincidence, from the experienced Hannah.

These were the days before Viagra and many were the fanciful remedies proposed for inspiring action from tired and under-performing husbands.

Hannah's close contact with the much-travelled Americans had inspired her to read a book about world travel, and her imagination had been particularly stimulated by a colour picture of an Indian snake charmer.

"He set thare aside a little ow barskit a-blowin' a flute," she had told Liza. "An' that ow snearke wus a-risin' up outa thet thare barskit all streart an' strong an' swayin' about.

"I reckon yew shud larn ter play the flute," she had advised. "Then one night orl yew're gotta dew is git Jimma ter sleep on his back. Yew set aside o-tha bed an play yar flute an see if the searme sorta thing happen ter Jimma."

A few days later the two women met again. "I tried yar snearke charmer trick," Liza told Hannah. "I set a-playin' the flute aside o-tha bed an' Ow Jimma never wook up, but my hart yew shudda sin the bedclooths start to rise up. I whipped 'em back an' blast me if his pyjama cord wunt standin' up streart an' strong an' swayin' about! I can't see what good that dew anybody."

Hannah was not too sure whether or not to take Liza seriously. But then, Liza was like that. You could never tell, neither from the expression on her face nor from her tone of voice, whether she was being serious or gently pulling your leg.

"I reckon we orta hev a little holiday," announced Jimma finally. "What yew might call a second honeymune."

"I dornt wanta go t'America," declared Liza emphatically. "But I wouldn't mind a-gorn ter Lunnon, just the once. They tell me thare's a lot ter see up thare, an' that int quite so far away as America. We can go by trearn."

So Jimma went to see Huby to book the train tickets. "Hang yew on a minnit," said Huby. "Dew yew're a-gorn ter Lunnon, jist yew come round an' see Hannah. We hed a letter from har twin brother Billy about twetty yare ago. That might hev some directions in thare what might tell yer how ter git about the plearce."

Round at No. 1 Railway Cottages Hannah was delighted to hear about Jimma's London trip. "To be trewthful," she said."Yew might be earble ter dew me a bit of a fearvour.

"Yer see, my brother Billy ha' bin down Lunnon twetty-odd yare. He never did write much of a letter an' we're worried about 'im.

"Dew yer think yew could go an' look 'im up? The larst address we hed for 'im wus Piccadilly W.C. One."

"Piccadilly W.C. One?" said Jimma. "I reckon thass a easy enough address ter remember."

The following Saturday Jimma and the Gal Liza set out for their great adventure. It was the first time they had ever caught the train from the main line station to London and they were, to say the least, excited.

The train rushed past fields of growing crops and through stations, stopping only occasionally before it ground through the suburbs of London and finally came to a panting, breathless halt.

Jimma opened the carriage door and got out on to the platform. Looking around him, he said: "Blast me, look at all these hare people. An' Lunnon's a site bigger plearce than what I thought that wus a-gorn ter be. Thass all covered wi' glarss."

"Dorn't talk so sorft," said Liza, heaving their suitcase off the train and standing beside him. "We int orf the stearshun yit. This hare's Liverpule Street. Thet ent our little ow village stearshun, yer know."

"Anyway," she added. "Fang yew a-howd o' this hare suitcearse. I aren't a-gorn ter carry that all over Lunnon."

Further along the platform, as they passed a sign saying "London Underground", Jimma remarked: "Blast me, fancy hevin' trearns runnin' underground. Where dew yer reckon all the smoke go?"

"They ent proper steam trearns," explained Liza. "They're 'lectric."

"Well ent that a rummun," observed Jimma. "I shouldn't want to hatta keep a puttin' shillins in their meter. I bet they dornt harf use up a lotta jewse."

The conversation carried on in much same the vein as they travelled by taxi to their hotel to leave their suitcase. "Thass a duzzy grit ow plearce, Lunnon, ent it?" marvelled Jimma.

He also found it was a more expensive place than he had expected, and the fare for the taxi, added to the cost of two nights at the hotel, used up all his spending money.

"What are we a-gorn ter dew?" he asked Liza in some dismay. "We hent even got enough money for the train fare hoom. We're stuck hare in Lunnon. I can't think o' much warse than that."

"Well," said Liza. "Thare is one thing I could dew if we're really desperate. Somebodda towd me once that in Piccadilly all a woman ha' gotta dew is stand about in the street an' men keep a-wantin' ter give har money."

"Well, thass a rummun yew should mention Piccadilly 'cos thass where the boy Billy Dunn live, so Hannah say," said Jimma. "I reckon we could booth go there an' yew could gorn git some money time I'm a-lookin' out fer 'im."

They set out to walk to Piccadilly. It took them some time, and they went a long way round, but they eventually found the place. Although confused by the traffic and overwhelmed by the noises and sounds of a busy city, they guessed they had reached the correct destination from the pictures they had seen in magazines.

"Orl right," Liza said to Jimma. "We're found Piccadilly. I'll go orf now an' git some money time yew find out where W.C. One is."

"Orl right Gal, but dew yew mearke sure an' tearke yar umbrella. That look like rearn," advised her husband, looking up at what he could see of the sky. With Jimma's advice ringing in her ears, Gal Liza disappeared into the crowd. Liza was, as has already been hinted at, a cunning soul with a wicked sense of humour. She was not as hard up as she had allowed Jimma to believe.

Before coming away for the weekend she had conducted a thorough search for Jimma's biscuit tin, and having finally located it in Bertha's sty, she had "liberated" £100.

She knew Jimma was a "mean ow skinflint" and had prudently hidden the money in her handbag just in case he ran short. Now, all she wanted was a little time to explore the marvellous sights and sounds of London on her own without the distraction of Jimma's inane conversation.

Meanwhile, for Jimma, finding W.C. One sounded easier said than done. He saw a policeman and decided the best thing to do was ask for directions.

"Excuse me Officer," he said politely. "I'm lookin' fer Piccadilly W.C. One. I're found Piccadilly but can yew tell me where W.C. is, please?"

The policeman looked at Jimma with amusement. Here was a country bumpkin if ever he (the policeman) saw one. He could have a bit of fun here. He was to regret giving way to the temptation to make fun of a "country bumpkin". It led to a chaotic sequence of events which caused an international incident and the loss of his job.

"Piccadilly W.C.One," said the policeman thoughtfully, sounding as if he was trying to be helpful. "Well, I can only think W.C. must be down there."

He pointed to a square of railings almost surrounding a flight of stairs which led downwards into a dark abyss beneath pavement level.

"Ent that the Lunnon Underground down thare, where trearns go?" asked Jimma, trying to sound as if he knew something about the big city.

"Don't worry," the policeman assured him. "There certainly may be dangers lurking down there but at least you won't get run over by a train."

Slowly and tentatively Jimma descended into the unknown. A sign which indicated that the place was reserved for "Gentlemen" at least reassured him that the people who lived down those stairs knew their manners. "They can't be tew bad," he thought to himself.

The stairs opened out into a dingy tiled area beyond which was a long row of doors. A gloomy looking man was listlessly pushing a broom across the floor, moving the litter from one side to the other and then back again.

"Blast if this ent a rum ow plearce ter hev as yar address," thought Jimma. "I dornt think I should want ter live hare. But there y'are; there ent no accountin' fer tearstes."

Jimma approached the attendant. "I s'pose this hare is Piccadilly W.C.," he remarked conversationally. The man looked around him without much interest. "I suppose it is," he agreed.

Pointing to the row of doors, Jimma asked: "Can yew tell me which one o' them's number one?"

The man took a long look at Jimma. "Why should you want to know?" he asked. "'Cos I're gotta a message fer sombodda what might live thare," explained Jimma unconvincingly.

The man's eyes narrowed. This was a time when the Cold War was at its height. Russian spies were everywhere and here was a strange man speaking in a funny accent and wanting to leave messages in public toilets.

At length, pointing to one end of the row, he said: "Well, if they were numbered I suppose that one would be number one."

As Jimma offered his thanks and moved off towards the door indicated, the attendant dropped his broom, hurried to his little office, grabbed a telephone and dialled a number.

Jimma knocked politely on the door of "Number One". Nothing happened.

He knocked again and heard the sound of running water and tearing paper from the other side. The door opened slightly and a man's head appeared. "What do you want?" it asked peremptorily.

Jimma was momentarily nonplussed by the deeply suntanned appearance of the face under a close cropped thatch of curly hair. Hannah and her brother could not have been identical twins! But he pressed on with his mission.

In the background the attendant emerged from his office, produced a camera and pointed it in Jimma's direction. MI6 would need photographic evidence, he thought.

"Are you Dunn?" Jimma inquired of the occupant of "number one".

"Yes, though I don't know what business it is of yours," replied the man with rising anger.

"Well, dew yew write hoom ter yar pore sister!" said Jimma firmly. "Thass what she're arst me ter tell yew an' thass why thass my business!"

At that moment there was the sound of running feet on the stairs. A pack of burly plain clothes policemen converged on "number one". Two of them grabbed Jimma, another two hauled the dark skinned "twin" from the cubicle and two more immediately began searching the pan and the cistern for hidden messages. Protesting loudly, the two men were dragged upstairs, bundled into cars and rushed to MI6 headquarters, where they were interrogated in separate rooms.

"That maniac wanted me to write to my sister," protested the former occupant of "number one". "She lives in Jamaica and I only spoke to her by telephone yesterday. I shall protest to my consulate about this outrageous treatment at the hands of the British Government! This is racial harrassment."

Meanwhile, a strong light was being directed into Jimma's eyes and he was protesting: "I hent never hard o' the Kay Gee Bee. What the hell is that? I'm jist a simple blook from East Anglia what wus a-dewin a fearvour fer a friend. This ha' gotta be that thare rearshul harrassment I're read about!"

The interrogator turned to his colleague and said: "I can only believe that "sister" is a code name for this man's secret contact, and the so-called Gal Liza must be his bureau chief, judging by the deferential tone he uses when speaking of her.

"Send a team to his hotel to search his luggage. There may be a weapon there; perhaps a poisoned blade disguised as an umbrella. These agents can be so devious these days."

The story of how Liza returned to their hotel to find four burly men ransacking their room and sorting through a suitcase containing her "unmentionables" is too awful to be recounted in detail for sensitive readers.

Liza could be formidable when roused - and she was definitely roused now. She brandished her umbrella angrily. The men cowered, especially when the point was thrust in their direction.

It took some hours of painstaking interrogation - plus the intervention of a uniformed policeman, who had to admit that he had directed poor old

Jimma to Piccadilly W.C. One out of mischief - before the cloak of suspicion was lifted from our hero.

It also took a close examination of Liza's umbrella, plus a letter of apology from the British Prime Minister to the Jamaican ambassador before the diplomatic incident was finally brought to a close.

The attendant at one of London's public conveniences received a letter from his employers congratulating him on his vigilance but warning him to be a little more circumspect in future before calling in Special Branch.

However, as a reward for his conscientious approach to his job, he was advised that he could have a holiday "at his own convenience."

Which explains the strange sight which greeted the "Gentlemen" who availed themselves of his facility the following week. The broom had been laid aside and the attendant was to be found in his office, reclining in a deckchair and sipping a cool drink!

The price the Metropolitan Constabulary had to pay was the loss of one uniformed policeman, who was sacked and had to find another job as a taxi driver, and a letter of apology from the Police Commissioner for London to Ow Jimma and the Gal Liza.

They had it framed and kept it on their mantelpiece for the rest of their married life. "That'll jist remind us how shanny city people go when they meet up wi' people what are diffrent to them," said Jimma to the Gal Liza after they got home. "Especially when they carnt unnerstand the lingo!"

"Mind yew," he added speculatively. "Fancy Hannah hevin' a twin brother what wus black. I wonder if Ow Billy ever did write ter his sister!"

Oh, an' by the way," he added, almost as an afterthought. "How much money did yew git given ter yew when yew stood in the street in Piccadilly?'

"Thirty-four pound ten shillings,' replied Liza with a wicked little glint in her eye.

"Bugger me," exclaimed Jimma. "What misrable ow skinflint gi' yew ten shillin?"

Liza grinned. "Thay orl did!" she said.

Chapter 13 - **A Play on Words**

Jimma and the Gal Liza had been together for many years. Now was the time for a second honeymoon. But it didn't work out quite as they had hoped.

"The trouble is," said Jimma. "That wunt much of a second honeymune. That wunt what yew moight call a relaxin' holiday what might ha' give us time ter put a bit more romance inter our marriage like what yew want.

"I'll tell yer what I'll dew Gal. I'll see if I can find the money fer us ter hev a little outin' ter the theatre in Norwich. That'd mearke a chearnge, an' yew never know but what we moight see suffin romantic what might gi' me a bit o' inspirearshun!"

Liza had a moment of concern over the thought of Jimma delving into the contents of his biscuit tin and finding them £100 short. But she need not have worried. He simply extracted the tin from beneath Bertha's protective bulk and gave his "hoard of gold" the most cursory of glances as he extracted just enough money to take them to Norwich by bus, and to the Theatre Royal.

There was no time like the present. Jimma had thought up the idea of going to the theatre and it had to be done right now, before he forgot. He had not got as far as consulting the local newspaper to find out what was on.

It was only after he had booked the tickets that he discovered that what was "on" was a three-act romantic comedy. "But yew might not unnerstand orl onnit," said Liza somewhat patronisingly. "Yew int much of a one fer plays."

"Yew'll enjoy it an' thass orl what matter ter me," her husband assured her with an unaccustomed touch of romance.

So they went to the theatre for the first and only time in their lives. The lights went down, and amid an atmosphere of rising excitement the play started. For Jimma, the evening went downhill from that moment onwards.

The first act went on, and on - and on. His head nodded forward, his eyelids drooped - and suddenly the lights went up to the accompaniment of much enthusiastic applause.

Jimma stood up. "Blast that wus good an' that dint larst tew long neither," he said, trying to sound enthusiastic.

"Set yew down, Jimma," said Liza in a hoarse embarrassed whisper. "That ent over yit. Thass only the end o' tha fust act!"

"Well, I're gotta mearke a call o' nearture anyway," said Jimma. "I better be a-gorn."

Politely Jimma passed along the row, treading on a number of toes and saying "Excuse me" to each of its other occupants as their seats tipped up to let him pass.

He got to the back of the auditorium and searched diligently, but unsuccessfully, for a sign saying "Gentlemen". He knew that was what posh people called the privy. He had seen the sign somewhere before - in London.

He went into the foyer - still no sign. But there was a commissionaire, a large and portly man resplendent in a uniform dripping with gold braid. "Blast he're got a posher uniform an' more medals than even Mussolini hed!" thought Jimma to himself.

He approached this imposing figure of authority and whispered: "Can yew direct me ter the Gents, please?" The man pointed to a corridor. "You go along there, down three steps, turn right, turn left and you come to a passage," he said helpfully. "The door you want is the third on the left."

Jimma went along the corridor, down three steps, turned right and left - and got completely lost.

By this time he was becoming quite desperate so, seeing a door that looked promising, he opened it, poked his head through the doorway and looked around furtively.

Before him, bathed in a pool of bright light, was a stretch of lawn in the middle of which stood a tree. Beyond was a lush green hedge. Dazzled by the light and in some physical discomfort, he took another look around him and saw nobody.

Pausing momentarily to reflect that some people were very wasteful in floodlighting their gardens, he tiptoed across the grass towards the tree. He was vaguely aware of a figure gesticulating wildly in the darkness, but he was in desperate need of relief by now and could not spare the time to investigate. The air seemed to be filled with disembodied laughter. He knew not from whence it came.

Moving behind the tree, he began unbuttoning his trousers. The laughter increased, verging on the hysterical as Jimma's puzzled face peered out from behind the tree. Where on earth was this strange sound coming from? All he could see beyond this odd pool of light was a pitch black void.

At that moment all hell broke loose. The lights went out abruptly and Jimma was dimly aware of the disembodied laughter crescendoing to fever pitch as he was surrounded by men clad all in black. They grabbed him and bundled him unceremoniously into the outer darkness.

A door opened and fresh air hit his face as he was ejected from the theatre. "Hold him down," said the stage manager. "I've already called the police." Turning to one of his assistants, he added: "I've seen it all now. Some people will do anything to get on the stage. Perhaps it's some kind of publicity stunt."

A few minutes later a police car screamed to a halt and out jumped two eager young officers. "Got 'im this time!" shouted one of them triumphantly.

Then to the stage manager and his team, still pinning Jimma to the ground, he added: "Well done lads. We've had reports recently of a 'flasher' plaguing young women, though I must admit he usually commits his crime in a dark alley, not on a brightly lit stage.

"Still, you can't get more public than that. We need an arrest and there are certainly plenty of witnesses."

"I'm arresting you on suspicion of committing an indecent act in public," said the policeman to Jimma. "You'll have to accompany us to the station to be interviewed by our duty inspector."

The policemen took charge of Jimma, bundled him into their car and screamed off to the police station. Again he found himself being interrogated.

Vainly he protested his innocence. "Carnt yew perlice think o' nothin' better ter dew than keep on arrestin' me?" he asked. "Orl I wanted wus a noice quiet evenin' at the theatre wi' my missus."

"If that was all you wanted, why did you make such an exhibition of yourself?" countered the inspector. "And what do you mean by asking if we can't think of anything better to do than arrest you. Have you been in custody before?" "Corse I hev," said Jimma, making matters worse for himself with every word he uttered. With instructions to his two subordinates to: "Keep an eye on this one," the inspector left the room and went to consult the criminal records department.

Looking up Jimma's file he read: "Theft of potatoes, one week in jail; conspiracy to steal mop whilst causing a disturbance on the high seas, two weeks; arrested in London lavatory on suspicion of spying, not charged."

It was certainly a strange and colourful record, but it pointed the inspector towards one inescapable conclusion. Jimma was nothing more than an accident-prone idiot.

He returned to the interview room just as a red faced sergeant burst in, hotly pursued by the Gal Liza. "This woman says we've got her husband in custody. I hope we haven't because she's going crazy."

"I'll hev yew lot fer harrassment o' innocent idiots!" shouted Liza, turning to the inspector, as the obvious figure of authority, and belabouring him about the head with her umbrella.

"Orl you lot keep a-dewin' on is arresting my Jimma an' I'm fed up wi' orl on yer. He hint never dun nothin' wrong. He hint got the sense ter be no crinimal. He's tew sorft in the hid!"

Jimma watched proudly as the formidable Gal Liza went into battle on his behalf. He was not too sure that the grounds on which she had chosen to base his defence, namely his complete idiocy, were entirely complimentary. But if anybody was going to get him out of this jam then Liza would.

"Get this mad woman off me!" the inspector shouted at nobody in particular. Then, more calmly to Jimma, and with a trace of sympathy in his voice: "Can this really be the woman you were hoping to spend a quiet evening with at the theatre?"

The two policemen held Liza's arms, receiving a few glancing blows from the umbrella for their pains.

"Now, please calm down madam and let us deal with this matter in a civilised way," implored the inspector. Liza subsided into a seething silence.

Then Jimma had a bright idea. "I can pruve I int no flasher," he protested vehemently. "Jist yew arst that feller what stand afront o' the theatre wi' orl thet scrambled egg orl over 'is cap. He's the one what gi' me the wrong direckshuns when I arst him the way ter the Gents."

"Thare y'are!" shouted Liza. "I towd yer he wus tew bricks short o' a lood. He carn't even find his way ter the privy wi'out needin' direckshuns. Thass a wunder the silly bugger can undo 'is trousers without me ter help 'im! Dew yew lot tearke us back ter the theatre an' arst that feller out the front dew he reckernise my Jimma."

Inspector, policemen, Liza and Jimma returned to the theatre where the commissionnaire looked hard at Jimma and agreed he did recognise him.

"I think I must have told you to turn left when I should have said right," he explained apologetically.

"That hint no good yew a sayin' that now, is it?" protested Liza. "That mearke yer wonder where people are a-gorn ter end up dew yew dunt know yar left hand from yar right. Look where thatta landed my pore ow Jimma."

The inspector decided to resolve the issue by releasing Jimma on the grounds of insanity, advising the commissionnaire to be more accurate when asked for directions, and giving Liza an official caution. "I hope you realise I could have arrested you for assaulting a police officer," he said. "So don't do it again."

"Dornt yew go arrestin' my Jimma agin then," said Liza, still proudly defiant. "I certainly won't if I can help it," muttered the inspector as he and his men returned to the police station.

By this time the play had ended. The theatre doors opened and the audience emerged. "Good, wasn't it," said a young woman to her boyfriend. "Yes," he replied. "But the funniest bit was when that tramp came on and started to relieve himself behind the tree. It certainly added something to the plot!"

Jimma turned to Liza. Polite as ever, he said: "When I arnswered the call o' nearture I dint 'spect I wus a-gorn ter be away so long. I'm sorry about that. What wus the second act like?"

Liza heaved a sigh of resignation. "Yew orta know," she retorted. "Yew wus in it!"

Chapter 14 -

Passport to Heaven

Jimma's unintentional appearance on the theatre stage had landed him in trouble with the law - again!

Jimma's one and only appearance on stage had finally convinced him that the world outside his own village held too many dangers for him ever to venture far afield again.

Trips to Lowestoft, London and Norwich had all resulted in our reluctant hero falling foul of the law. His life had been eventful enough without tempting fate by travelling to "furrin" parts any more than was absolutely necessary. He would, for ever more, stay in his own village.

Liza would always be the first to acknowledge - and Jimma the second - that their life together had lacked a certain romance. Ow Jimma had been an awkward, rather than a passionate, spouse.

Now, as Young Jimma and Jemima - with the aid of their partners - began giving them grandchildren, Liza reflected that all she had left, by way of passion, were memories - and they weren't up to much anyway!

Jimma's old friend Jarge, on the other hand, had made what the world would regard as a success of his life. Everything he had touched had turned to gold. He had property, land and money. He also owned the "big house", former ancestral home of the late Lord and Lady Wymond-Hayme. But he also had a demanding wife.

From her earliest days Letitia had nursed ambitions of marrying into the aristocracy. However, unable to land an earl, a duke or even an "honorable", she had settled for a self made man.

She might well live in the "big house" but wealth was no substitute for breeding, and even now she entertained hopes that a "gentleman" would take her into the upper strata of society to which, she felt, she naturally belonged.

To help these hopes along, she "latched on" to Felix, the former butler at the "big house", who seemed to know all the right people.

She spent much of Jarge's money on improving her wardrobe, and started accompanying Felix to hunt balls, point-to-point race meetings, horse shows and gymkhanas - all places where she fondly believed "the gentry" gathered.

Felix, his pockets lined with the money Jarge had paid him for the "big house", also had ideas above his station. He and Letitia were an ideal partnership.

She had become tired of Jarge, his pedestrian ways and his motto: "Hard wark never hart nobodda!" In turn, he felt uncomfortable with the new friends his wife had acquired. While she went out he stayed at home.

Spending so much time alone, he decided to put it to good use. He bought a dog and trained it carefully to come to his call, walk to heel and guard his property.

Many years before, his friend Jimma had given him a young parrot. He had claimed that it had emerged from one of the three eggs he had bought from a pet shop near Norwich market.

He had been attracted to the shop by a magnificent talking parrot which sat on a perch outside. The shopkeeper had professed himself unable to sell the parrot, but had sold him "three of his eggs" instead.

In truth, the birds which emerged when Jimma hatched them in the oven of his kitchen range, did not resemble parrots. But, reluctant to admit he had been fobbed off with duck eggs, he had bought a parrot from some gipsies who had passed through the village.

He had lived to regret the purchase. With the Gal Liza and two growing children occupying his own small home and his mother living next door, he had come to the conclusion that: "there's enough sqwarkin' a-gorn on around hare wi'out hevin' a ow parrot chippin' in as well!"

So he had given the parrot to Jarge who had named it Archibald, in memory of his wife's father (whom he greatly disliked), and had used the time he spent alone painstakingly teaching the bird to talk.

The parrot proved a quick learner and Jarge taught it well. After a few months it knew most of the swear words in Jarge's limited vocabulary - which tended to outnumber the respectable ones - and could recite one or two of the more earthy East Anglian folksongs which Jarge remembered from the days of his youth when they had regularly been sung in the tap room of the Pig and Whistle.

One night, after Jarge had gone to bed, and was safely away in dreamland, a dark and sinister figure came lurking around the house trying the downstairs windows.

One of them was not properly fastened. It slid silently open and the burglar found himself in the room which the pretentious Letitia knew as the "withdrawing room" and Jarge insisted on calling the "parlour".

Even in the soft moonlight which came in through the open window the burglar seemed to have an uncanny knowledge of the layout of the room.

He moved silently over to an elegant 18th century bureau and began opening the drawers, convinced that many good things of great value were to be found there.

Suddenly the stillness of the night was broken by a strange scratchy voice, almost a hoarse whisper. "Jesus is a-watchin' yew," it said quietly in a broad East Anglian accent.

The burglar, at heart a superstitious man - at least where his own safety was concerned - whirled round. He could see nobody. Was the place haunted? Was some protective spirit calling on the Highest Authority for help? The voice certainly sounded inhuman, if not exactly supernatural.

Silence reigned. The moonlight shed a ghostly glow over most of the room but it also left dark impenetrable shadows. "There's no voice," said the burglar to himself. He had been imagining things.

Again he turned to the bureau and opened another drawer. "Are yew deaf, yew sorft ow bugger?" asked the same unearthly voice. "I now say Jesus is a-keepin' his eye on yew, an' yew dint pay me no heed. Dornt yew say I hint warned yer!"

The man whirled round again. If this really was a ghost, it was the first one he had heard of that swore. In a momentary flight of fancy, he thought: "I suppose you could call that 'ghoul' language."

But another soft sound banished all bad jokes from his mind. It was a kind of snuffling, heavy breathing sound and it came from right behind him.

Again the burglar whirled round. Again he saw nothing. Again the voice broke the stillness of the night.

"Bloody hell!" it said, more loudly this time. "Yew dunt harf tearke a lotta convincin'. I tell yer Jesus is a-watchin' on yer!" The man took his torch out of his pocket and shone it in the direction from whence the voice had come. The beam picked out a parrot sitting on its perch.

The burglar swung the torch around again. No, there appeared to be nobody else in that part of the room. The voice must have come from the parrot. He moved gingerly towards it.

"Did you just say that?" he asked. "Say what?" retorted the parrot. "Did you just warn me that Jesus was watching me?"

"Corse I bluddy did, an' thass trew an' orl." "You're a very clever bird," said the burglar, suddenly thinking that the parrot could conceivably be the most valuable thing in the room. "What's your name?" he asked in a tone of voice which suggested that it might be a catch question.

"Archibald," replied the parrot. "That's a daft name for a parrot," remarked the burglar, growing bolder now.

"That int harf as darft as callin' a bluddy greart Alsatian dog Jesus!" countered the parrot. The remark suddenly reminded the burglar of the heavy breathing sound he had heard coming from behind him.

At the sound of his name Jesus leapt forward and sank his teeth into the man's backside. There was an unearthly yell - and this time the burglar knew exactly where it came from.

There was also a sound of rending trousers as the intruder set off at a speed which would have won him an Olympic 100-metre medal, hotly pursued by the barking Jesus.

Upstairs Jarge leapt out of bed, grabbed his 12-bore shotgun, flung open the bedroom window and let fly. There was another unearthly yell from somewhere in the grounds.

Deeply wounded, both in anatomy and pride, the burglar sped home. Next day the local doctor had a visit from Felix, the once proud man who had been butler at the big house in the time of Lord and Lady Wymond-Hayme.

"That's a nasty wound," said the doctor as the butler bared his nether regions. "How did that happen?"

"A shooting accident," muttered the patient vaguely.

"Strange," remarked the doctor. "The gun appears to have left teeth marks. God knows how that can have happened!"

"Actually, God may not know," whispered the butler, painfully and almost inaudably. "But Jesus certainly does!"

When Letitia heard about the incident she was outraged. All her sympathy was with Felix. When Jarge came home early from a tour of his properties one day and caught them in the master bedroom, the butler minus his trousers, she upbraided her husband for having a suspicious mind.

"I'm tending to this poor man's wounds," she said, accusingly. "Why der yew hatta tearke yar clooths orf as well then?" asked Jarge reasonably.

"If you are going to behave like this I am leaving you," shouted Letitia, a little too loudly, Jarge thought. She promptly dressed, packed her new wardrobe and went to live with the butler.

"Good riddance ter booth on yer," said Jarge. The truth is that he had not been spending all his time teaching the parrot to talk. During his tours of inspection around his properties he had caught the eye of young Molly, still a lively and generous daughter of the former Little Edie and still single.

She was also ambitious and the thought of getting her hands on Jarge's money - now that he also appeared to be single and had no heirs - far outweighed any concern she may have had about the considerable difference in their ages.

She moved in with Jarge at the "big house". He was entranced by her youth and beauty, and flattered by her attention. But the presence in his life of someone so young and lively served to remind him of his own mortality and the passing of the years. So he decided to visit the doctor for a "medical".

"You seem to be wearing out fast," said the doctor. "Perhaps the pace of life is too much for you!" Jarge took the warning to heart. It was difficult to put the brakes on the pace of life with Molly around, so perhaps he should check his spiritual wellbeing.

He called on the Vicar. "What dew yer reckon my charnces are of a-gorn ter Heaven when I die?" he asked. "Well, we must first explore your way of life," began the Vicar. "Do you smoke?"

"Well, I're gotta be honest, Vicar, I dew. About forty fags a day an' a nice big cigar arter dinner," replied Jarge. "You must stop that at once," counselled the Vicar. "There are no ashtrays in Heaven. Do you drink?"

"Well I dew like my Southwold beer an' I dew hev a tidy few pints onnit, 'specially at weekends," admitted Jarge.

"Well you should cut that down," warned the Vicar. "They don't like drunkards in Heaven. And what about, ahem, (he cleared his throat discreetly and lowered his voice), the pleasures of the flesh?"

"Say what yer mean, Vicar. Yew mean sex," declared Jarge. "Well, I wunt a-gittin much o' that time Letitia was around, but things ha' perked up now I'm wi' a younger woman. She're got what yer might call a big appetite."

"Fornication is banned in Heaven and you must curb your carnal desires," declared the Vicar. "Now, I have given you three challenges. Come back to me in three months time and we'll see how you are getting on."

The three months seemed more like three years to Jarge as he tried his hardest to give up the three things he enjoyed most in life.

"How did you get on?" inquired the Vicar when Jarge arrived to make his progress report. "What about cigarettes?"

"I're give 'em orl up," reported Jarge proudly. "I hent hed a fag since I saw yew larst toime." "Well done," said the Vicar. "And beer?"

"Yis, I're gone on the wagon. I hent hadda pint since we larst met." "Good for you," said the Vicar, beaming encouragingly. "You're at least two-thirds of the way to Heaven. Now what about the final third, the, ahem, sex."

"Well, I wus hully dewin well till the other day," explained Jarge. "That little ow gal o' mine wus a wearin' a little ow short skart an' she wus a-bending over the 'fridge an', well, I got overcome wi' lust an' we hed a little session there an then. Sorry Vicar."

"Oh, what a calamity!" exclaimed the Vicar. "And you had been doing so well, too. I'm afraid they won't allow you in Heaven after that unfortunate lapse."

"I dorn't s'pose they will," agreed Jarge ruefully. "They wunt allow us in the Co-op no more neither!"

It was a matter of deep regret that Jarge was unable to meet all three of the challenges set him by the Vicar. In fact, his morale sank so low that he not only did his best to keep up with Molly; he also went back to his favourite East Anglian beer.

And a year or two later Jarge, the late developer who had made a personal fortune without ever mastering the skills of reading and writing, passed peacefully away.

Well, perhaps not exactly peacefully for, as he lay in the master bedroom at the "big house", Molly bent over his bed, anxious to hear his dying words.

"Orl this hare'll be yars now," he whispered. "Orl what I're warked for. I wish yer well with it 'corse yew're mearde me hully happy. Mind yew, I dornt know what my charnces are o' gorn ter Heaven. At least I did manage ter give up smookin'."

As his voice grew fainter Molly bent over further. "Oh, what the Hell!" he suddenly exclaimed. With a last supreme effort he flung his arms around her neck, planted a huge kiss on her lips - and promptly expired. But there was a lovely smile on his face.

Chapter 15 -

Cycling into the Sunset

In her younger days Mother had a marvellous new bike. Jimma kept this ancient machine in his shed and rode it into town to collect his pension. The expedition again ended up with him "helping the police with their inquiries".

Times were changing fast in Jimma's village. His mother had passed on and his old friend Jarge would by now have discovered whether a place had been reserved for him in Heaven.

If there was he would have been certain to meet up with Farmer Greengrass, Huby, the teller of tall tales; Sid, the old pub landlord; and even Canon Gunn, who had all been promoted to the everlasting pastures.

There were no horses on the farm now. There were not many workers either. Many hedges had disappeared and huge combines dealt efficiently with the harvest.

It was time for Jimma to retire. His decision never more to travel far from his village seemed ironic now. He had never learned to drive a car. The village shop and pub had closed, the railway had gone and the bus service, such as it was, took you into the nearest market town on Thursday but did not bring you back until Saturday. Such was progress.

Three things stopped Jimma and the Gal Liza from becoming prisoners in their own home. They could still walk; which meant they could still enjoy the countryside and its wildlife, which they had loved all their lives. They could also visit the village Evergreen Club each Wednesday afternoon and get to the service which took place on alternate Sundays at the village church.

They could still cycle, and both still had their "(t)rusty steeds"; sturdy old "sit up and beg" bicycles which had been built many years before to ensure sedate progress rather than speed.

And their daughter and son-in-law still lived next-door to keep an eye on them and take them out from time to time in their car.

Farmer Greengrass, that kindly old "marster", had left the two cottages to Jimma and the Gal Liza in his will, and Jimma retired soon after the old man died. He couldn't face the idea of working for a new boss anyway.

He still had his cottage garden to look after, and with a river running conveniently through the village, he had taken up fishing.

One day, as he sat beside the river watching his float, an empty tin by his side, a boat full of holiday tourists pulled into the bank and moored.

To all appearances, Jimma was asleep, his head nodding forward, his mind dwelling on happy memories of an eventful life. "Look at that poor old yokel," said one of the holidaymakers. "He's been nowhere, done nothing, and he looks as if he hasn't got two pennies to rub together, poor old sod."

Taking pity on the apparently poverty-stricken old fisherman, the holidaymaker walked up to him and placed a pound coin in his tin. Then, pausing, he concluded that the old man might be lonely. He would engage him in conversation - and maybe poke a little fun at him. He wouldn't know. He was too simple, of course.

"Have you caught many today?" the holidaymaker asked in mock-friendly tones. Jimma pocketed the pound coin, looked up at the stranger, smiled his gappy smile, and said: "I reckon yew're about the fourth!"

Puzzled, the holidaymaker returned to his boat while Jimma's gaze fell back to his float. "I'll put some bait on my 'ook one o' these days," he thought. "Mind yew, wi' orl these hare genrus holidaymearkers about I can afford to go to town and buy me fish!"

On the day after he finished work Jimma cycled into town to go to the Post Office and claim his pension. Years later he was still telling the tale of how the Post Office clerk thought he was too young for a pension book. But that is a story we will get to shortly. Other things happened before he got home from that eventful trip into town.

Having visited the post office he decided to call at one of the pubs in town. The beer flowed and the landlord was in conversational mood.

Jimma had always delighted in poking gentle fun at pub landlords ever since he first suspected that Sid, former genial host at the Pig and Whistle, had enjoyed a "fling" with the Gal Liza.

The talk in the town pub turned to antiques. "I dew loike antiquews," said Jimma expansively. "Dew yew know marster, I're gotta special antiquew back hoom in my shud. I inherited that from my father an' thatta bin in my family for generearshuns.

"Thass a owd axe," he continued. "Dew yew know, thass so owd thatta hed ter hev tew new handles and three new hids!"

The landlord nodded sagely. It was always difficult to tell whether East Anglians knew they were having their legs pulled since their faces rarely betrayed emotion of any kind. And anyway, the beer was beginning to have its effect on both of them.

"I loike fishin' an' orl," said Jimma. "Dew yew know I caught an ow pike in our river th'other day an' that musta weighed fifty-five pound if that weighed a ounce!"

"That ent nothin' much," said the landlord. "I can tell yew a story what'll cover booth yar interests - anteeks an' fishin'

"That happened like this hare. I went sea fishin' orfa Southwold beach th'other day. Now, if yew're read yar history yew'll know there wus a battle thare hundreds o' yare ago 'twin the English an' the Dutch when they only hed sailing ships. The Battle o' Sool Bay they called it.

"Dew yew know what?" continued the landlord. "I thought I'd caught suffin hully big an' blast me when I reeled in my line I found the 'ook hed got caught up in a lantern orfa one o' them ow sailin' ships. An' yew can believe this or not, but that wus still aloight!"

"Dornt talk so sorft!" exclaimed Jimma. "That wouldn't ha' stayed aloight orl them hundreds o' yare in the sea. That'd ha' runned outa paraffeen!"

"What I'm a-tellin on yer is trew!" slurred the landlord indignantly. "No that ent," returned Jimma. "Thassa packa lies."

"Orl roight then," countered the landlord. "I'll dew a deal wi' yer. Dew yew tearke ten pounds orfa yar pike an' I'll gorn blow my lantern out!"

When Jimma finally emerged from the pub and mounted his bike, he was decidedly unsteady and having difficulty resisting the temptation to sing loudly and tunelessly.

As he wobbled off down the road a sign at the local garage caught his eye. "New car wash" it proclaimed. "I wonder if they dew bikes an' orl," thought Jimma.

He cycled unsteadily into the garage, paid his money, put it in the machine and watched entranced as the water spouts started and the brushes began to whirl. Sitting proudly on his bike he was washed, lathered, rinsed and dried.

As he emerged the garage proprietor, who had been watching the process with interest, remarked: "Is this your first time in a car wash?" "Yis," replied Jimma.

"I thought that was," concluded the garage man. "We dornt git many threw hare on bikes!"

"Well yew should dew," responded Jimma, still under the influence of the ale he had imbibed too freely in the pub. "Thass verra refreshin'. I're hed a barth an' that dornt happen any tew often!"

With that he cycled off, dripping wet and leaving a wobbly trail behind him.

Whether it was the drink, or whether it was the effect of soapsuds getting in his eyes we shall never know, but Jimma failed to notice the policeman who stepped out into the road in front of him - until it was almost too late.

Becoming vaguely aware of a stout figure standing firmly in his path, Jimma took avoiding action. He swerved; his front wheel hit the kerb and he careered across the road to the bank on the other side. The bike mounted the bank and, as Jimma fell backwards, his machine landed on top of him.

"I suspect you're drunk!" said the policeman, bending over and wagging a warning forefinger at the recumbent Jimma. "'Corse I'm drunk," exclaimed our ageing hero. "Yew dunt think I cudda dun that sober dew yer?"

As Jimma accompanied the policeman to the station he reflected that it was certainly not the first time in his life that he had been required to "help the police with their inquiries."

The first the Gal Liza knew of Jimma's predicament was a call from her daughter Jemima who lived next-door and whose home - unlike that of her parents - had a telephone.

"Father's in trubble agin!" she shouted over the fence after taking the call from the police. "They say we'd better go at once; he's a-gorn ter be uncondishunly discharged, or suffin."

"How can he be discharged?" exclaimed Liza. "He int no gun."

"Dornt be so sorft," shouted Jemima. "That mean he's a-gorn ter be let orf!"

"Well thare y'are!" replied Liza. "We better gorn git 'im then afore some harm come tew 'im."

"We better hurry 'cos the perlice say they carn't put up wi' him keep on singin' loike he dew. The people what live next ter the police stearshun ha' started complainin'," reported Jemima.

Arnie was called from the bottom of the garden, where he was planting a row of 'tearters, and the three jumped in his car and went off into town to collect Ow Jimma.

The sound of singing from the police station's single cell had been replaced by snoring by the time Jimma's rescuers arrived.

"Tearke him hoom," said the desk sergeant. "I dew know that int no good a-chargin' on-him. He'll never larn whatever we dew tew 'im. Anyway, that involve tew much pearper wark."

Nothing surtprised Liza about Jimma after all her years with him, but even she was a little taken aback to find him wrapped only in a regulation police towel.

"He wus sookin' wet," explained the sergeant. "He reckoned he'd hed a barth but I carnt think where nor yit why he kept his clooths on. Anyway, where-ever that wus, they're got some funny smellin' barth salts."

So they took Jimma home and he slept the night through. Next morning Liza started on him. "I spose yew dornt remember what yew went inter town for yisty!" she said. "Dornt yew keep a-mobbin on-me gal," said Jimma. "I're got the skull earche."

"Sarves yew roight," said his wife unsympathetically. "Yew shunta got drunk."

"I wus only celebreartin' arter I'd bin ter the post orfice," said Jimma. "That there gal ahind the counter wouldn't gi' me a pension book at fust on account o' she dint think I looked owd enough fer one."

"Oh ah," said Liza with some scepticism. "How did yew convince har yew wus?"

"Well I undone the buttons on my shart an' showed har the gray hairs on my chest. That convinced har," explained Jimma.

"Blast bor, thass a pity yew dint undo yar trouser buttons 'cos dew yew hadda dun yew mighta got a disability pension an' orl!" quipped the still unsympathetic Liza.

"I jist mighta got meself arrested agin, as well," retorted Jimma. Perhaps he was starting to learn the errors of his ways!

They were back on the subject which had provoked more discussion during their married life than any other - sex and Jimma's general inadequacies in that department.

But never mind; they were still together, progressing gently towards the sunset of their lives, fortified by their shared experiences, their memories of a slower, gentler age - and their love for each other.

Oh yes. They may never have actually said it - and that word "love" may not have figured prominently in this narrative. But Jimma and Liza certainly loved each other - and they always would.

"She hent bin a bad ow gal ter me orl these yare," thought Jimma romantically as he retrieved his biscuit tin from the pigsty and put in what remained of his first pension payment.

Other East Anglian titles available from
Nostalgia Publications

TITANIC - THE NORFOLK SURVIVORS
John Balls
The stories of the five Norfolk survivors of this historic disaster

WYMONDHAM - A CENTURY REMEMBERED
Philip Yaxley
A chronicle of the town's history over the past 100 years

THE HOBBIES STORY
Terry Davy
Over 100 years of the history of the well known fretwork company

LARN YARSELF NORFOLK
Keith Skipper
A comprehensive guide to the Norfolk dialect

LARN YARSELF SILLY SUFFOLK
David Woodward
A comprehensive guide to the Suffolk dialect

LARN YERSALF NORTHAMPTONSHIRE
Mia Butler and Colin Eaton
A comprehensive guide to the Northamptonshire dialect

LARN YARSEL ESSEX
Richard Thomas
A comprehensive guide to the Essex dialect

KID'S PRANKS AND CAPERS
Frank Reed
Nostalgic recollections of childhood

RUSTIC REVELS
Keith Skipper
Humorous country tales and cartoons